Jason Summers

CW00435137

Warranilla

By Jason Summers

For Hannah & Rue

Prologue

The crunch of gravel, the flash of car headlights, and muffled voices were all Nick remembered of the night of February 5th, 1992. The night his mother was killed.

The loud cries of his father from their bedroom woke him the next morning. Opening his eyes, and looking across to his little sister Jess sleeping, he could feel that something was very wrong.

Getting back early from an unsuccessful shooting trip, Nick's father, Tim Vada, had walked through the front gate of the family home. Finding it odd that despite the warm weather the insect screen and front door were wide open, it wasn't until he saw the blood-soaked footprints in the hallway and on the front porch that he broke into a run, screaming, 'Billie, Billie!' at the top of his lungs.

He burst through the hallway sliding door and ran through the dining room, over the upturned dining chairs strewn throughout, and towards the master bedroom at the back of the house, not even thinking to stop into the front bedroom and check on his two kids who he knew were in there.

Coming to a stop at the door and seeing the blood-soaked footprints at the entrance, he braced himself for what he thought may be inside.

'No, Billie, please God, no!' he cried as he gazed into the bedroom.

There, lying across the bed on her back, lay his wife, Billie. He could see through her blood-soaked white nightgown that she had been stabbed multiple times. Her lifeless eyes gazed up at the ceiling.

Chapter One

He smelt it before he saw it, the distinct smell of a canola crop coming through the vents of his car. Home, he thought to himself quietly, with the smell of the crop bringing back many memories of a mostly happy childhood, except for that one big event.

Coming over the rise and past a 10km sign full of bullet holes, Detective Sergeant Nick Vada looked out across the vast flat stretch of paddocks and further on towards the rice silos of his hometown. A farming town, Milford had once been a small pub and post office where horse-drawn carriages would stop on their way through to the main cities. Expanding due to the rice and wheat farming which started in the 1930s, it soon grew to be a large, thriving township, with bustling shops, pubs, and was full of tourists enjoying the river which ran through the outskirts of town.

Looking down at his fuel gauge, he noticed the yellow caution light alerting him that he was nearly out of fuel. He hated his new European police car, which only showed 'fuel low', instead of how many kilometres were left until empty. How was he supposed to know when he was about to run out of fuel?

Changing the station over to the local channel, he listened in, hoping for some news of substance. He got news about a date change for the local show and a weather report. 'Seven days ahead of clear skies with temperatures reaching the high 30s.' Great, he thought, he certainly wasn't used to the hot dry weather of the bush after his eight years in the city.

At 38 years old, he no longer felt young enough to be considered cool with the younger crowd, and not old enough to be considered experienced. After a rough year in Sydney, on a particularly bad missing person's case, he felt like the trip back to his hometown could be refreshing. After breaking up with his last girlfriend a few months earlier, he felt like his only ties left in the city were his work colleagues, with most of his other friends being more the friends of his ex, Monique's than his. Being from the bush, he never truly felt like he fit in with the latte-sipping, activewear-clad friends of his ex.

His childhood in Milford had been a mostly pleasant one, with days spent swimming in the river, playing sport, and spending time with his Dad and his sister Jess. He couldn't help but smile, thinking how his little sister was finally getting married. Having no motherly figure in her life growing up had made things hard for both of them. When his mother was murdered Nick felt like he took on the role of another parent, due to his Dad being so busy working to keep money coming in. The family had never been wealthy like some of the other kids who had owned farms back when the town was thriving.

Nick's mother, Billie Vada, had been killed in 1992, in what they described at the time as a 'vicious and cold-blooded attack.' With Nick and Jess being at home at the time, he had had recurring nightmares for the past 30 years of his life, of blood-stained walls and screaming voices. He tried his best to mask the nightmares with a laser-like focus on his career, with not much time left for anything else. He felt guilty heading back to Milford, as he rarely made the long drive down from Sydney, and knew that his old friends and family were always disappointed in his lack of visits to town.

Nick loved Milford and always felt like it was a part of him, but the recurring nightmares of his mother's murder were never far from the back of his mind. Coming back to Milford always made them come to the forefront. He had memories as a kid of the hushed tones and whispers of people who would look at him in the streets, always with a small sigh and a shake of the head at the loss of his mother. 'Such a waste,' they would mutter under their breath at Nick, who at that time was too young to understand.

Lifting his gaze from the horizon, he looked up in his rear-view mirror to the unmistakable flashing of the red and blue lights of a low slung and menacing highway patrol car. He was surprised he'd made it this close to town without being pulled over by the local highway patrolman. He flicked on his indicator just before the faded, 'Welcome to Milford' sign, and felt his tyres leave the smooth asphalt and bump down into the rough table drain.

The tall highway patrolmen exited his car slowly, walked down to Nick's car and lightly tapped on the window. Nick pressed the button with a grin.

'The prodigal son returns.'

'Jack, mate, you been well?' Nick said.

'Of course, young fella, just trying to keep the local roads safe.'

Standing in the bright sunshine was Jack Thomson, Milford's local highway patrolman for the past 20 years. Tall and thin, with a shining bald head and piercing green eyes, Jack cut an imposing figure of authority. Not the typical figure for a highway patrolman, Nick thought, as he remembered his overweight colleague Paul Jensen back at his local station in Sydney, always with a large McDonald's frappe in hand and something sweet close by. Jack's long tanned arm resting on Nick's car door still showed signs of the muscles he had back in the day as Milford's best footballer and also their long-standing coach. When Nick was younger, he remembered Jack taking Milford to their one and only premiership. With the whole team on his back, he kicked the winning goal after the final siren. The whole team celebrated for a month afterwards. A close friend of Nick's father, Tim, he had served as a second father for Nick and one of the reasons he had initially decided to join the NSW police force.

'Thought I'd be seeing your car sometime today. Only three more sleeps until the big day. Can't believe our Jessie girl is finally tying the knot!'

'Yes, it's been a long time coming,' Nick said. He had known her soon-to-be husband fairly well during his youth, but was caught quite off guard when his sister discussed marriage after a whirlwind romance. He certainly didn't seem her type, he thought.

'Dinner at six tonight at the Coachman's Inn. If you feel like a pre-wedding beer mate. Nell and I will be there.'

Nick's mind cast back to the old pub in Milford. In the centre of town, it was the last pub left that hadn't closed down along the main street. During the eighties and nineties, the three grand hotels were all in hot competition for the farmer's and families' affection, and more importantly, their money. The Marlin was the first to go in the year 2000 due to the elderly owners passing away. He always wondered where the name had come from, with the closest ocean being 400 kms from Milford. It wasn't exactly a nautical town.

The Globe Hotel was the second big casualty, with the drought in 2003 being the death knock. He remembered that time well, as it was when he left his hometown to join the police force.

'Thanks, Jack, I'll keep you posted.'

Flicking the indicator stalk on the right-hand side and setting off the windscreen wipers, Nick cursed at himself. The new European car was not the same as the Australian-built cars he had enjoyed over his policing career. With too much technology, he found himself missing the simpler Holden cars that the detectives were given when he started. Making his way back onto the highway, he slowed at the 60km sign at the entrance to Milford and sighted the local farm supply store to his right, with only one solitary ute parked out front. Driving further along the main highway past the only surviving local motel, he couldn't help but remember all the thriving businesses before the big drought had hit. With a population of over 15,000 when he was growing up, Milford had dwindled down to 3,000 these days. Businesses had closed due to a myriad of issues. The young were moving away in droves to the big cities for schooling and then deciding to stay as failed crops, and government policies controlling the water supply, slowly killed the farming community.

Turning into the local fuel station, he noticed a couple of young kids on BMX bikes loitering around beside the garage, smoking and playing on their phones. Different times these days, he thought to himself. If his old man or Jack caught him smoking back in the day, there would have been hell to pay.

The eldest of three yelled out, 'Nice car, mate.'

'Thanks,' Nick replied, as he opened the fuel flap on the side of the BMW. $1.89 a litre. Jesus, Head Office will have a fit when they see that in the monthly accounts, he thought. He was glad he had a fuel card.

The eldest rolled over casually on his bike, with a vape pen in his left hand. Where this vaping had come from all of a sudden was a mystery to him, but he knew from chatting with colleagues in the drug squad that it was becoming a vice for a lot of young kids and an easy gateway to drugs.

'Shit's bad for you,' Nick said to the young teen.

Blowing a puff of smoke that looked similar to a steam train, it covered the back half of his BMW in a grey mist. 'We're all gonna die one day,' the teen said as he rode off. Charming, Nick thought, wishing he could show them the effects of the harder drugs kids in the city were doing after starting out on the vapes.

Clipping the fuel flap closed, he ran his eye over the old petrol station. Faded red signage advertised fresh fishing tackle and roast beef and pork specials each Friday night. A BP service station in his youth, Nick now wasn't sure what company it belonged to, with a mismatch of red painted windows and green signage out the front, almost giving the old building a Christmas theme.

Pushing open the glass doors with a creak, he noticed the once-pristine building was now much older and dirtier than he remembered. The cracked linoleum floor had footprints leading from the door to the main register that had almost been worn into a pattern. In the corner, a frozen coke machine displayed an 'out of order' sign, and the pie warmer lay empty.

'Just the fuel love?' said the shop attendant, Julie Mason. Overweight and in her 70s with half-moon glasses sitting on the edge of her nose and a grease-covered apron, she sat on an old red bar stool at the register. Everything within her arm's reach.

Julie and her husband Earl had run the local service station for as long as Nick remembered.

'Yes, thanks, Julie.'

Recognition lit in Julie's eyes and a small half smile curled on her lip. 'Nick Vada! Gee, you've grown a bit since I last saw you. Here for the big wedding?'

'Wouldn't miss it.'

Chapter Two

'Killer of multiple women finally caught.'

'Jim Hooper finally put behind bars.'

Nick's first few years in the police force were spent obsessing over news articles and reports of one of Australia's most notorious serial killers, Jim Hooper. In a spree spanning 16 years, it was said he had murdered over 18 women across two states. It was almost one a year.

A brute of a man, many of the women had been found viciously beaten and sexually assaulted, with a telltale sign being the breaking and entering of the women's homes to commit the crimes. Jim targeted young single women who were in the prime of their lives, snuffing them out before they had even really begun. His exploits throughout the district were well known, with locals in many towns still claiming to see him wandering the streets at night in small country towns.

Hooper was finally caught and arrested by legendary detective Jason Peters. Nick hoped that one day he could sit down with the now elderly detective and talk to him about his own mother's murder, and pick his brain to see what he knew, or whether he saw any connections.

The murder of Edithvale woman, Jen Walker, in 1994 was an almost carbon copy of his own mother's murder, and he had managed to view that case file and see similarities, with the main difference between the murders being the savage beating of the Edithvale woman.

Looking further into Jim Hooper's background, he knew that he had sheared on multiple farms surrounding his hometown of Milford, and it was well known he had drunk in the local pub, the Coachman's Inn. Legend has it, he got into an argument with a well-known local footballer at the time, beating him so savagely that he never set foot on a football field ever again.

Whenever Nick's mind turned to his mother's murder and his hometown, Jim Hooper's smiling mugshot was always at the front of his mind; with a sneer suggesting he was shocked it had taken so long to catch him. As Nick made his way through the years in the force, he always dreamed that one day he could look deeper into the case and finally put an end to his family's pain.

When Nick was a kid, he had this recurring fantasy of becoming a policeman and solving his mother's murder. As he worked his way through the ranks and finally became a detective, he slowly realised that with such a lack of evidence, and no DNA or forensic material collected, the likelihood of pinning his mother's murder on Jim Hooper was next to zero.

With no forced entry into the home, police initially looked at Nick's father, Tim, but he had a rock-solid alibi of being out all night shooting with his friend Gary Jones, so he was quickly struck off the list.

It's not like the house would've been locked anyway, thought Nick, knowing that his parents always left the front and back doors of the family home open. Friends and family were always welcome, his mother used to say.

Nick's Dad, Tim, had grieved in his own silent way, like all Australian men did in those days, but Nick knew back then and still to this day, that he could never love another like his Mum. Once all the news and gossip about his father around the town had finally died down, Nick and his little sister Jess had a relatively trouble-free childhood, with his dad trying his best to keep them on the straight and narrow despite being away for long stints as a shearer. Nick's grandmother Kath was his rock for those tough years, with days spent at her house eating her famous scones and helping her to tend to her roses in the garden.

Nick indicated left and turned into the local motel, the Milford Inn, and pulled his car in towards the front reception. Long and low with beige coloured bricks and dark brown windows and doors, the motel was well overdue for a renovation, considering it was one of the first things you saw coming into town. As he got out of his car, he yawned, tired from the long drive from Sydney. Looking across the carpark, he could see the gaping cracks in the hot bitumen and long brown weeds sprouting out of them. There didn't seem to be a lot of maintenance out here anymore, considering they would be struggling to remain open. As he walked over towards the glass sliding door, he shooed flies away from his bottom lip. Flies and heat were two things he didn't miss about home.

'How many nights you in for?' asked the motel clerk. A young man in his early 20s, he had a long greasy ponytail and wore thick-framed black glasses and a stained and ripped grey Metallica t-shirt. Nick noticed his computer screen had Facebook open, and a thick fantasy novel lay half read on the counter.

'Make it three,' he said, as he slid his credit card and driver's licence over the counter.

'Hmm, Vada,' said the clerk, holding up his licence and reading the information. 'Here for the big wedding, I assume?'

He wondered if anyone in this town hadn't heard about the wedding. 'Brother of the bride,' he replied.

'She's marrying into money, that's for sure. I wouldn't mind becoming a Waterford.'

Nick thought back to his youth and his days spent out on the Waterford's farm and time spent with his father growing up.

'Some would.'

He grabbed his driver's licence and credit card and made his way slowly down past the old dark green plastic tables and chairs set up in front of each room. The sun was beginning to lower itself down in the late afternoon and the reflection of sunlight off the motel windows glared into his eyes. It's only November, he thought to himself, remembering how hot January and February could become in his old hometown.

Walking up to the faded door with a crooked number 6 on it, he slid his key into the brass door knob. There wasn't a swipe card in sight as he walked into the dimly lit room.

When he slid the musty pale blue curtain back it revealed exactly what he would have guessed: dark brown carpet, brick-lined walls, and a small double bed, with a cover that looked like it hadn't been cleaned in 10 years. There was a small table and chair; a desk running across the side wall housed an ancient TV, and a phone and tiny bar fridge sat underneath, with an old refrigerated air conditioner clicking into life in the back wall beside the bathroom. It certainly wasn't luxury, but it'd have to do.

His phone rang from inside his pocket. 'Hello?'

'Nick, Jack here mate, don't forget dinner at the pub at 6. Nell hasn't shut up about seeing you since I got home.'

'I'll be there, Jack.'

He sat on the edge of the bed and thought about the old pub. Trying his best to stay away from alcohol after some rough patches in his childhood and earlier days on the force, he knew that it would be hard to stay away from temptation back in his hometown, with his mind wandering to the small fridge under the old tv.

Tentatively opening the door, he found just two small bottles of rum and vodka. Cracking the rum bottle, he lifted it up to his nose and took a deep breath; as the smell transported him back to a time with his little sister when they broke into his Dad's stash and sipped from the big bottle with a yellow label for the first time. Taking a quick swig and downing the whole small bottle in one hit, he hoped he could control himself while he was in town, as his mind raced back to mistakes made in the past.

Taking a quick shower to freshen up, he put on his best casual clothes and pocketed the small bottle of vodka, feeling his strong determination and willpower he usually held in the city leaving him. He held solace in knowing he wasn't currently on a case, so what harm could a few drinks be?

Walking down the long gravel driveway and into the cooler air of the evening, he took a deep breath and smelt the fresh country air. Dead still, with only the sound of a few stray cockatoos flying towards the river and the hum of the main highway, he always felt uneasy in his hometown. Like an outsider not feeling like he truly belonged here, or in the city.

He made his way slowly down the highway and came to an intersection where the main street began. Turning at the corner of a closed and boarded up shop, he knew it once housed a thriving café which was the busiest in town, full of families and tourists eating brunch and drinking coffee's it now lay dormant, with a 'closing down' sign faded, and covered in cobwebs in the front window.

The Coachman's Inn was the main local pub in town with the classic wrap around double storey veranda that all country towns in New South Wales seemed to have, well past its glory days, it was painted a now dust coloured light grey with white trimming. Walking under the large top floor deck and looking up at the old, pressed tin ceiling, he noticed huge gaping holes in the once grand ceiling, now home to many families of pigeons, the footpath was covered in bird droppings. The pub had gone through many owners throughout the years, with the last owners from the city deciding to pour a truckload of money into it, they gave up 5 years ago, and it was finally closed.

Being reopened by the long-time bar manager and now owner, Marty Kelly, Nick had many memories in the old building, being the pub he had his first beer in at 16 years old. Rules didn't seem to apply back then, and he smiled to himself thinking back to the many long summer nights he had spent up on the top balcony with his friends as a younger kid, sneaking a couple of liquor bottles away from the publican, while his Dad drank downstairs with his mates.

The unmistakable smell of beer tipped on carpet, a loud jukebox playing AC/DC, and the clinking of pool balls had him smiling for the first time in a few weeks as he walked through the front doors on the corner of the building. Walking through the main bar, he spotted Marty the publican standing behind the taps with a warm smile on his face and a drying towel draped over his shoulder.

'Evening Nick, Long time,' he said. Marty had managed the Coachmans for many years, and after years of uncertainty, had finally decided to buy the pub for himself. Now in his late 60s,

Nick felt like there wasn't a time he had been in the old building without Marty perched behind the bar with a warm smile.

'Evening Marty. Drink for the long traveller?'

Lifting a beer glass up to the frosted taps, the seasoned barman poured a perfect beer and placed it up on the red gum bar. The cool glass glistened, and he felt a tingle on the back of his tongue in longing of the amber liquid.

'$4.50, thanks mate,' Marty replied, passing the now wireless EFTPOS machine over the bar towards him.

He thought about the advancements in technology in his childhood pub looking at the wireless machine and chuckled at the incredibly cheap prices, with a pot of beer in his local pub in Sydney costing him more than double the price.

'Wouldn't hurt to bump that price up Marty and give this place a spruce up.'

Marty laughed, pointing towards the end of the bar at the line of old bar fly's sipping on cold drinks. 'I'd lose half my customers. Here for the big wedding, I assume? Talk of the town.'

'Yep,' he replied, taking his first sip of beer, feeling the cold liquid fizzing down his throat, he already felt lighter on his feet with the slight buzz of the rum kicking in.

'You had much to do with Pete Waterford these days?' Marty asked, speaking about his sister Jess' soon to be husband.

'Haven't spoken to him in at least 15 years, I'd say.'

Marty picked up a fresh beer glass and began to polish it thoughtfully. 'I won't say too much, but keep an eye on him, mate.'

'Thanks, Marty.'

'He's not causing any trouble, is he, Marty?' Jack Thomson yelled over Nick's shoulder, walking in their direction.

'Not at all, Jack,' Marty smiled. 'You going to sort those Bears out next season?' he added, referring to Milford's local football club.

'I've been asked to coach, but I really need to think about it,' Jack laughed. 'Might be getting a bit old for that.'

'Bullshit,' Marty scoffed. 'You were the best country footballer I've ever seen.'

'Keep that up and his head won't fit through the door,' replied Jack's wife Nell, smiling at Nick and Marty, as she walked into the conversation.

Nick turned and gave Nell a warm hug. Tall and slender with long shining grey hair, Nell Thomson and Jack had been childhood sweethearts. Local netball coach, and schoolteacher, she had been like a second Mum to Nick as he grew up. Kind and always caring, she was well loved throughout the community and always attentive to a younger Nick's emotions.

She looked the detective up and down with her usual motherly stare, unable to have children, she had always treated Nick and Jess with a sincere kindness, trying her best to fill the void left by his mother's passing.

'You looking after yourself, Nick?' she asked.

He finished off his first beer with a quick sip, with his eyes set on another. 'Always Nell.'

'Keep an eye on that. Nothing good comes from it.'

'I know, I know.' He was a grown man, he thought. I can control myself.

'Nell, sorry to hear about your mother.'

'Oh, it's no worry, Nick, she had a good run. I hope I live till I'm 95!'

'I don't,' Jack cut in, laughing at his wife. 'These knees already kill me, and I haven't even retired yet!'

Walking through the main bar and into the bistro, Nick looked around. It hadn't changed since his last visit. Dark red carpet adorned the floor and also the walls, with paintings of old ancient Chinese landscapes plastered everywhere. A long-ago renovation, four owners earlier, had decided that the pub would have a Chinese restaurant. Marty had decided to leave it, preferring to spend his money elsewhere. After ordering dinner at the bar, the three made their way in and sat down at a table for four.

'Excited for the big day?' Jack asked Nick with a wry smile on his face.

'If Jess is happy, I'm happy, mate. I'd just like to know how she's ended up marrying a Waterford on your watch!'

'Well, you've been gone now for a long time, so it's been hard keeping an eye on her. She's really happy mate; the happiest we've ever seen her.'

Through the odd phone calls and texts, Nick's sister Jess had kept him up to date on her whirlwind romance with Peter Waterford, son of Russell Waterford, one of the region's biggest landowners and owner of half of the buildings in town. Pete was two years younger than Nick and had gone away to boarding school for his schooling life, but from memory, Nick thought he was that same farm boy turned private school kid who thought he was better than everyone else. What Jess found in him was news to him, but he thought he should try to get to know him better, considering he was about to join the family.

'I'm glad.'

'Mate, your Dad hasn't been going too well lately. Not sure how much he's told you, but looks like his cancer may be back.'

'Really? Jess hasn't mentioned much. I haven't spoken to him yet.'

Nick had a falling out with his dad when he left to join the police force. He had always resented the fact that Nick had left him and his little sister. Time had healed some wounds, but he knew their relationship would never be the same.

'Well, I guess you'll see him at the wedding anyway,' Nell said, with a sad smile on her face.

After dinner, he paid at the main bar and began to make his way out when he saw her. Standing at the end of the bar was Jemma Revell, his high school sweetheart. Tall, athletic, and tanned, she had sparkling green eyes and long black hair, which hung down at her shoulders. She looked the same as she did the day Nick decided to leave Milford and join the police force. As he walked through, on his way out, he caught her eye and gave her a wave.

'Long time no see,' Nick said in her direction.

'I thought I would be seeing you here,' she said with a smile.

'Here for the big wedding. Any gossip on the groom? Never thought my sister would marry a Waterford.'

'He's certainly cleaned up his act from back in the day. He's not the boy you remember.'

'Well, as long as Jess is happy, that's all that matters,' Nick said, surprised at just how gracefully his old girlfriend had aged. He couldn't say the same for himself, with his hair greying at the temples and the effects of alcohol making him soft around the middle.

'You still taken these days?' he asked.

Jess's friend, sitting beside her, turned to look at who she was talking to. Red wine in hand and eyebrows slightly raised, she cut in.

'Hi Nick,' she said, holding out her hand.

Nick couldn't believe his eyes. Smiling at him was Trudy Young, Jemma's best friend.

'Trudy?' Nick replied, looking at her up and down for the first time in astonishment. 'You look a million bucks!' he commented, not believing how much weight she had lost.

'Thank you. I own the local gym now.'

He almost laughed at the thought of Trudy Young owning the local gym. She had once been twice the size she was now. He couldn't believe how good she looked.

'To answer your question, no, sadly work comes first at the moment,' Jemma cut back in. 'I don't have time to think, let alone have a partner. What about you? I'm sure a famous detective like you would be spoilt for choice?'

He knew that Jemma would have heard of his recent breakup through the local grapevine and wondered just how busy a shop owner could be in Milford these days, after seeing the multiple boarded-up shops on his walk over.

'Nope, I'm the same.' He smiled in her direction, sipping his beer. Trying to count what number he was up to; he didn't really care at that moment. 'What about Dean?' he replied, knowing she had had a long-term partner.

'Dean left to work in the mines and decided to stay, so it's just me and Mum now above the shop.'

'Oh, sorry to hear,' he said, thinking he wasn't, really; Jemma's partner Dean was always a bit of a dickhead.

'That's all right. You should come past the shop Monday before you leave.'

'I definitely will. Another round?' he asked, finishing off his drink again. Slow down, he thought.

'Sounds good to me.'

Talking about their old school days, the three of them caught up drinking and laughing, the years apart faded away like it was nothing, He never felt like an outsider when he was with Jemma, and he wondered whether one day he could call Milford home once again.

After a round of rum and cokes, Jemma and Trudy decided to call it a night. 'Thanks, Nick, it was great to see you.' He could still feel the chemistry in the air. 'I hope I see you again before you go.'

Watching the two women leave the bar, he decided on a nightcap. 'One more Marty.'

Marty raised an eyebrow at him and walked over to the fridge with his back towards the detective, wisely filling his glass with just coke.

He sculled the cool drink down and let out a burp. 'Thanks, Marty.'

'No worries, mate,' Marty replied, hoping his young friend would get home safely. 'You need me to call you a cab?'

'Nah, I'm right, I'll walk,' he said, almost tripping as he got off the barstool, he made his way out of the pub into the cool night air.

Making his way slowly back to the motel, he cursed himself for drinking too much, knowing that he was going to feel the effects tomorrow morning. Unable to bounce back from drinking as well as when he was younger, he knew he would be no good until at least lunch time.

Walking into the entrance of the motel and fumbling his keys in the door of his room, he was temporarily blinded by the bright lights of a white work ute as it accelerated out of the car park. He was unable to make out the sign written on the side of the ute or catch the number plate. They looked like they were in a hurry.

Falling through the door and onto the rock-hard bed, he soon fell into a deep, drunken sleep.

Chapter Three

Owls hooted in the night air, high in the gum trees lining the river, and the moon cast bright light across the old waterway, which was etched into the landscape millions of years ago. The centre of the universe for the surrounding wildlife, it was soon to be the place where one life was about to end.

As she sprinted along the old farm road, she had never felt so scared in her life. Hearing the loud vehicle revving its engine, she could almost feel the heat of the motor burning the back of her legs.

What was she doing? She knew she shouldn't have pushed the issue, but thought he would calm down. He always did. Now, as she ran down the dirt track, she felt true fear, unsure of what he was truly capable of.

'Please stop!' she yelled over her shoulder, as she felt the bumper of the vehicle clip the back of her feet as she ran.

Over the roar of the engine, she could hear the laugh of the driver, unhinged and manic. Seeing the gum trees rising in the distance, she thought she may be able to lose him down by the riverbank.

As she ran, she thought about her previous few months and all the stupid decisions she had made. She was due to go to university in a few weeks and hoped this night would just end, so she could crawl into bed until morning came.

Finally, making the trees, she cut between two massive trunks, hearing upset owls flapping off in the distance. Behind her, she heard the vehicle come to a screeching halt in a hail of dust. The bright moonlit night illuminated the figure as he opened the driver's door.

She had played netball growing up and had won a couple of cross-country races as a kid. Fit and healthy, she realised now with him out of the car she may, just may, stand a chance. Hearing him yelling and swearing her name, she could tell that he was extremely angry.

Getting to the river's edge and looking down towards the old pump station, she realised that the cover of gum trees shaded the area quite well and hiding might be her only chance. Hearing what she thought was the sound of the bolt action of a rifle, she felt a chill up her spine. She knew he had guns and wasn't afraid to use them. Would he truly go to that extreme?

Sliding to the bottom of the bank where the river met the cold dark water, she shivered in the blackness, only wearing a short dress and shoes not fit for traipsing across a farm. She didn't know how long she would be able to hold out here, cold and alone.

Making her way further down the sandy back, she sighted the end of a massive river gum. Roots gnarled and twisted at odd angles; she could see that the end of the old tree was hollow. Hoping she would fit inside, she raced to the edge and ducked under the thick, twisted branches.

Now sitting inside the hollow tree, she could no longer hear the sound of the person who she once thought she had loved. I was young and stupid, she thought to herself, as she held her hands over her mouth, trying to control her breathing.

Feeling her heart hammering in her chest, but with her breathing now under control, she sat in the old river gum and listened into the silence. The only sound was the cicadas chirping by the riverbank and the odd hoot of an owl. Trying to sense movement around her, she couldn't feel anything, and wasn't sure whether he was gone, or whether she was beginning to freeze in the cold.

A face popped around from under the tree branch, with eyes wild and a manic expression. A face of evil. 'Hello, sweetheart.'

'Please, no!' she screamed as she scrabbled further back into the hollow log, and she kicked her feet out in his direction.

Catching a glimpse of a shine in the muted moonlight, she realised he held a long hunting knife, with a smooth black handle and a menacing serrated edge.

Feeling a rough hand around her ankle, she was dragged kicking and screaming out of the old hollowed-out log. As her dress rode up over her backside, the harshness of the riverbank sand scratched the back of her legs.

As she was dragged past the pump station and into a clearing, she made one last desperate attempt to flee. Twisting in a clockwise direction, she managed to pry herself free from his grip. Planting her hands into the sand, she began to stand up, and tried to run away, but as she looked up at the riverbank, with the headlights of the vehicle at the top illuminating the horizon, she felt her head tilt upwards as he grabbed her by the hair.

She screamed out in pain as she felt tufts of her hair leaving her head. 'Ughhh. Please, no!'

As she was spun around, she felt a warm, rough hand wrap around her neck, tightening its grip ever so slowly.

'I should've done this weeks ago,' he said, with his black eyes showing no emotion.

Just as she tried to open her mouth to protest, she felt the long-serrated hunting knife enter her chest, as a burning, searing pain enveloping her entire body. As she fell backwards towards the ground, she saw him falling forwards towards her, his face full of glee in the dark night.

She tried to remain awake as she felt the knife enter her again and again, her whole body now feeling like it was on fire. She was sure she had never been in so much pain in her whole life.

Watching him stand up and hold the knife in the moonlight, she could see a piece of her dress attached to the blade. Looking down at herself she realised that her chest and arms were covered in blood.

As the figure began to walk away in the darkness, she lay back on the cool riverbank. Feeling the sand on her back, slightly warm with her blood, it almost made her feel better.

Feeling her eyes heavy, she thought of her Mum and Dad, and hoped they would find her in time. In case he came back.

A single tear fell down her cheek as she breathed her last breath. Her life on the riverbank now extinguished.

Chapter Four

Still asleep and with his head thumping, Nick heard his mobile phone ringing loudly in his jeans pocket. Slowly rolling over, he reached across and pulled the phone out, and answered.

'Hello,' he said, still half-asleep, wondering if he still may be drunk.

'Nick, it's Mark.'

He sat bolt upright, rubbed his eyes, and cleared his throat, trying to sound more alert.

Mark Johnson was the Detective Chief Inspector of the New South Wales homicide squad and was a legend of the force. He had helped mentor Nick during his formative years as a detective. He was sharp as a tack and well respected. He and his team had solved hundreds of murders throughout his career, and were a pivotal part in taking down Ivan Milat, Gregory Brazel, and Jim Hooper.

'Hi Chief, everything ok?'

'Nick, there's been a murder in Milford.'

He rubbed his eyes and face again, wondering if it could be
true. The last murder in his hometown had been that of his own
mother.

'I know you are there right now on family business, but I need
you, mate. Report to the local police station. I have informed
them you will be my man on the ground. Give me a call if you
require any assistance, and no bullshit Nick.'

'Yes, sir.'

He was surprised the Chief was going to let him run the case
alone. It would give him a good chance to prove himself after
what happened in Sydney last year.

He quickly got up and shaved, had a shower, and put on his
jeans and a shirt. He hadn't anticipated being on the job back in
his hometown and made a note to head down to the local shops
and buy a decent shirt and pants for work. Taking two Panadol
tablets and sipping from the luke-warm can of Diet Coke in his
cup holder while he drove, he made his way over to the local
police station. Walking down the narrow concrete footpath, he
almost walked headfirst into Jack Thomson, who was on his way
out.

'Jesus mate, you smell like shit,' he said, with a sour look on his face.

'Didn't quite expect I would be needed,' he replied, squinting at Jack through the bright sunshine.

'Where is everyone?'

'Warranilla.'

'Shit. Ok.'

Jumping back into his police car, he began to make his way out of town and out towards Warranilla, soon eyeing the main gates in the distance. As he turned in, he wondered what he was about to drive into.

Driving through the main gates of the Waterford's farm, 'Warranilla', he replayed happy memories of his childhood with his Dad. His Dad, Tim, had worked for Russell Waterford on and off throughout the years, and Russell had always allowed him to shoot rabbits and roos on the property.

Warranilla sprawled over 450 acres of prime land, with sections of the Edward River running in and out of it. The Waterfords had been one of the first rice farmers in the district in the early 1930s and had slowly accumulated more and more land through successive cropping seasons and now owned the largest property in the region.

Driving down the long gravel driveway with gum trees lining each side, ahead he saw the sprawling homestead which the farm was named after. Built in the 1920s and after multiple extensions, it was one of the most prestigious homes in the state. Federation style with a large feature front gable and wrap-around balcony all in white trim, Nick always thought it looked like it belonged in an upper-class suburb of Sydney.

Going past the homestead and following Jack's directions, he made the long drive towards the back of the property, where he knew the river cut through the furthest corner. Upon arrival, he saw the two local Toyota Landcruisers of the Milford police, a 4-wheel motorbike, and an old black Ford panel van which he knew belonged to the local doctor, Bruce Smith. He pulled in slowly and cut the engine.

Getting out of the car and into the warm morning, he could feel the alcohol beginning to seep from his pores. Wiping his brow and looking at the break in the gumtrees near the riverbank, he began to walk in the direction of voices.

Continuing down the shallow riverbank and towards a large river gum stretched out over the water, he saw a figure lying on the muddy riverbank. Blue and white police tape was wrapped around the perimeter of the scene and close by stood three people. Pulling his dark sunglasses down over his eyes, he hoped he could hide his hangover, knowing that first impressions counted in the bush.

The largest of the three men walked around toward him with an outstretched hand. 'You must be Nick? Senior Sergeant Jim Turner, call me Sarge.'

He wore a light blue NSW police uniform, and wore a black Akubra hat pulled down low over his dark brown eyes. The Sergeant stood tall over the two other people and had a round beer belly, making it look like his police shirt was about to pop. He wondered whether he would pass the fitness exam these days. His complexion was a light shade of red and Nick thought he must be quite the drinker, although who was he to talk?

'Also, this is Constable Joanna Gray,' he added, pointing to the short woman beside him. Standing at just over 5-foot-tall, she had short brown hair, smooth tanned skin, and a bright white smile.

'Pleasure to meet you both. Detective Sergeant Nick Vada,' he said, introducing himself. He shook both of their hands, hoping they wouldn't detect the smell of alcohol on him.

'The famous Nick Vada,' said Bruce Smith with a smile as he stepped forward, shaking Nick's hand with a firm grip.

'Read about that big case up in the city last year mate, great work.'

'Thanks Bruce, never thought I'd be out here investigating a murder,' he said, pointing down towards the body of the young woman. 'What have we got here?'

'Rose Perry. Twenty years old,' Bruce said, as he stepped under the blue and white police tape. 'Multiple stab wounds to the chest. Looks to me like it would've pierced the heart or very close to it. No signs of sexual assault and minimal defensive wounds, suggesting she knew her attacker.'

His mind raced back to the past as he looked at her body, unsure of what advantages could be made of his local knowledge.

'She was dragged. It looks like she was hiding over by that hollow log over there,' Bruce said, pointing over at a large river gum which had toppled into the water.

'Any relation to Matt Perry?' he asked, thinking of the Perry farm out the other side of town. He knew the Perrys and remembered his Dad drinking with Matt down at the local football club from time to time.

'His daughter,' Joanna said. 'They don't know yet.'

'Time of death?' Nick asked, as he stepped under the tape and assessed the body up close.

'I would say early last night Nick; her body is in the early stages of rigor mortis. Poor girl, I was only talking to her mother last week about her heading off to university.'

'Murder weapon?' Nick said, trying to keep the local doctor's mind on the job and focused.

'I'd say a large knife of some sort, probably a hunting knife.'

'Who found her Sarge?'

'Young farmhand, checking the pumps around 6am this morning. Got the fright of his life, of course,' he said, pointing down to the collection of large diesel pumps running out of the river, which were used to irrigate the farm. 'Russell Waterford called it in to me this morning.'

Nick wondered what the landowner would have thought as the young farmhand came screaming into his office, telling him of a dead body on his property. Certainly not your typical day out on the land.

'And do we have Crime Scene Services organised?' he asked.

'No, we don't,' the Sarge replied. 'They are tied up in Edithvale and have asked if we can assist in our own evidence retrieval.'

'Right.' Was all he could think to say in reply to that. Just how backward were things out here?

As he looked at the body on the hot, dry riverbank, he had flashbacks to an earlier time in his life. Although the white dress remained relatively unstained, the resemblance to his mother was almost uncanny.

Rose lay flat on her back. Arms spread out evenly, like she had just decided to have a rest. Except for the wounds. She had been beautiful: pale skin with auburn hair, and hazel eyes, staring up at the now blazing sun. He couldn't help but think she didn't look like she came from Milford. She looked like a model who could walk the catwalks of London or Paris. What a waste, he thought, once again thinking back to his mother, who had met the same fate.

Chapter Five

On one of Nick's visits back home when he'd first started in the force, he had decided to stay at Jack and Nell's home, due to the frosty reception his father had given him at the time. As Jack set off for the day on patrol, Nell tasked Nick with cleaning out their back shed to give him something to do.

As he slowly worked through the junk in Jack's shed, he found four small, neat archive boxes under the bottom bench. Pulling them out and wiping the dust off, he read, 'MILFORD POLICE' on the top of each box. Curious, he opened the lid, and was shocked to find a dusty manilla folder marked: HOMICIDE – Billie Vada. Shocked at finding the case file on his mother's murder, and making sure Nell wasn't looking, he slid the folder into the inside of his jacket and took it out to his car.

Unable to wait any longer, he drove his old ute down to the edge of the river near the caravan park and stopped and parked. Looking around to see if anyone was watching him, he wiped the dust off the front cover of the folder, and realised he had come across the complete case file and crime scene photos of his mother's death.

The photos were not something he ever thought he would want to see, but his training immediately kicked in before his emotions, which shocked him. Assessing each photo with a quiet contemplation, he wondered to himself just how thorough the homicide detectives in the 90s had been when trying to find his mother's killer, and why Jack Thomson had this in his possession.

'Any thoughts?' Joanna said quietly, snapping him back to the crime in the present.

He said nothing, thinking of all the people who could have seen the killer entering and exiting the farm, and thinking his first stop would be Warranilla, the Waterford's homestead.

'Feels like the ghost of Jim Hooper has been here,' Bruce Smith said, shaking his head at such a waste of young life.

'Well, we already got him, Bruce. He's not our problem anymore.'

'Nick, Joanna is welcome to join you if you need a second set of hands,' the Sergeant said from behind them.

'Thanks. Joanna, let's head up to the homestead.'

'Well, looks like the wedding's on hold,' said a voice from the top of the riverbank.

Tall and thin with a mesh trucker hat sitting on top of a thick tuft of light brown hair, Pete Waterford slowly made his way down the hill toward the crime scene tape. Hand outstretched, he walked to Nick first, and Nick noticed a bandage around his hand.

'Long time no see, Nick. Hope you've been well.'

'Pete, May I ask why you are entering an active crime scene?' he said, with the authoritative tone he usually put on when he was interviewing witnesses.

'I-uh, thought I'd better come and say g'day,' Pete said, taken aback by his tone.

'What happened to your hand?' Nick asked, pointing at the bandage.

Pete chuckled nervously. 'Ah, this? Cut it last week while I was fencing.'

Nick looked closely at the bandage with fresh blood seeping through the bottom of the dressing.

'Looks like it needs attending to.'

Pete looked down at his bloodied hand. 'Oh right, I must have knocked it earlier.'

'I'd suggest you make your way back to the homestead Pete. Constable Gray and I will be with you shortly.'

'No worries,' Pete said, waving off the unpleasantries and walking back up the riverbank. With the 4-wheel motorbike starting up, Nick heard him work his way through the gears and into the distance.

'Bit harsh on your future brother-in-law?' Joanna asked.

'Considering we have a body on his property, I would say he is a suspect until proven otherwise.'

'Fair enough.'

He helped Bruce load Rose into a body bag, and with the help of Joanna, they slowly made their way up the riverbank with the body on a stretcher. Bruce struggled with the weight due to his age and Nick wondered when his natural strength would slowly start to leave him. A top-rated cross-country runner in his youth, he tried his best to maintain his fitness, but as he got older, he felt like the alcohol was beginning to win. Never one to say no to a beer with colleagues or friends, he tried to maintain a healthy balance as best he could.

Pulling up slowly to the Warranilla homestead with Joanna's Land Cruiser in tow, he couldn't help but wonder how the Waterford homestead was maintained to such a high standard. With crisp white picket fencing across the front and sides, large pink and white camellias trees were trimmed neatly in rows behind it. The place hadn't really changed since his first memories of it when he was a kid.

Watering the camellias wearing a wide-brimmed straw hat, he realised, was none other than Samantha Waterford, the matriarch of the Waterford family. Ageing gracefully, she wore crisp light moleskin jeans with RM William boots, and a loose blue and white striped shirt, which covered her thin frame. He wondered whether she always did the gardening, or whether it was a bit of a show, knowing the detective and constable were on their way up to the homestead.

'Nick, Joanna!' she called out as they stepped out of their vehicles. 'Come in, please.'

Walking closer to Mrs. Waterford, he realised that she actually was beginning to get on in her years. She had aged considerably since the last time he had seen her. He wondered whether the years of drought had slowly started to get her.

'Thank you, Mrs. Waterford,' Joanna replied.

'Samantha, please, Miss Gray,' Samantha said in her sharp, almost English accent. Nick had always wondered as a kid if she was faking it.

'Samantha, hoping to ask yourself, Russell, and Pete a couple of questions,' Nick said.

'Of course. Russell is back in his office. I think Pete has headed across to the east shed to check the headers. I'll get him back here for you.'

Walking down the vintage clinker red brick footpath, and up onto the deck under the pergola to the main entrance, Nick looked at the impressive black front door with matching stained-glass windows on each side, "1929" was ornately pressed into the green and red stained glass. They certainly don't make them like they used to, he thought to himself quietly, as he thought of his modern, small townhouse in the city.

Following Samantha down the long hallway of light spotted gum floorboards, they made their way into the centre of the home, which was a spacious dining room, with the biggest dining table he had ever seen in his life. Made out of dark red gum and polished to a high shine, it had Warranilla etched into the end of it, and he couldn't help but wonder how often the 16-seat table was ever filled.

'Impressive, isn't it?' Samantha said, watching his eyes cross over the table. 'Made in 1930 by the original builders of the homestead. They used red gum from the very banks of the river that passes through our paddocks.'

'Too much cleaning for me. I'll stick to my 2-bedroom unit,' Joanna said, eyeing the expansive room.

'Mr. Waterford?' he asked, hoping to move things along.

'This way.'

Walking through the dining room and into a kitchen of the same impressive size, he marvelled at the size of the large red gum butcher's block bench. Above it, cast-iron pans and pots hung from a rack. In contrast was the row of stainless-steel induction ovens, cooktops, and industrial sized range hood across the back wall.

Heading left at a small hallway coming off the kitchen, and into the back section of the house, Samantha tapped lightly on the dark oak door. 'Come in,' boomed the deep voice from inside.

They made their way into an office with burgundy carpet and sunshine blazed through the two full height windows, and directly into Nick and Joanna's eyes. A sturdy red gum desk sat in the centre of the office, with family photos in silver frames sitting in each corner. Papers were scattered across it and a computer was nowhere to be found.

Sitting in the pressed stud leather chair across from Russell Waterford, was a young fertiliser agent wearing a bright red polo jumper and cream moleskin pants, deep in discussion with the elderly farm owner.

Russell spoke to him. 'Mate, if they drop our water allocation anymore, I'll be up shit creek. Last year was a disaster and if I get rain now, all it will do is help grow burrs.'

'I think the tide is changing, Russell,' the young agent said. 'Solar hasn't won yet.'

Russell scoffed. 'And it never will. We've been farming this land for 80 years and it won't be changing anytime soon.' He sighed and looked over at the two officers. 'Thanks Jeremy. Best I speak to these two now.'

Russell Waterford sat leaning back in his high-backed leather chair. In his early 60s with shining blue eyes, dark grey hair, and a moustache of the same colour, with his shirt sleeves rolled back, Nick noticed multiple sunspots and scarring across his hands from many years working in the hot sun. For all the hard work, he still looked fit and healthy, and could've passed for a man much younger than his years. He gave Jeremy a wave off before the young agent closed the door.

'Nick Vada, gee you've grown,' he said, with his deep voice booming across the room.

'Good afternoon, Mr Waterford, hoping to ask you a couple of questions about what we've found on the property.'

'Call me Russell, please. Oh, that. Yeah, Terry, my young fella found her around 5 this morning. He's out sweeping the machinery shed, if you want to chat with him. He was checking the pumps on the river line before the sun came up. Terrible shame, from what I hear; she was a pretty young thing.'

'She had a name, Russell,' Joanna interjected. 'Any unusual activity around here last night or early this morning?'

'Hmm, nothing I can recall. I was in town last night for a few meetings but was back home by 10. Sam and I had a bottle of wine on the back deck and were in bed shortly after.'

'And Pete?' he asked.

'Sam said she heard him get home around 11. In town with Jessie preparing for the big day,' Russell said, with a smile. 'Looks like that'll all be on hold until this business is cleared up.'

The way Russell was speaking, it was like this murder was some small inconvenience. "This business' is a murdered woman on your property Russell. This is extremely serious. I'd ask you to speak with your workers and see if they heard or saw anything unusual last night. Also, give Pete my number and tell him to call me.'

'Will do. You know, those cattle carters from out Turner's farm way are a dodgy mob. One of the boys said they saw one of their trucks flying past the farm late last night, well over the speed limit, mind you. I've spoken to Jack Thomson about them countless times and he's done nothing.'

'We'll look into that, thanks.'

He wrote down Turner's Transport in his notepad, knowing of the company Russell referred to from his childhood, and he remembered their huge stock crates ambling through town. With sheep and cattle on their way to slaughter, the smell was unmistakable.

'How's your old man?' he asked, as his features softened. 'Heard he was crook?'

'He'll be fine,' Nick said, as he felt his head beginning to throb. He didn't feel like talking about his Dad. 'Look, if you hear or see anything else, make sure you let us know, please?'

'Thanks for your time,' Joanna said.

'Anytime.'

Making their way out of the office and back out towards their cars, Joanna was the first to speak. 'What do you think?'

'Hard to say, I feel for them having a murder like this occur on their property, but something feels off with Pete Waterford. We need to talk to him as soon as possible. Did you see his hand? Hopefully, he can help shed more light on it.'

Walking back out towards the cars, Nick sighted a young farm worker sweeping out the shed beside the homestead. He could feel alcohol once again seeping out of his pores, and he grabbed a piece of chewing gum from his pocket and put it in his mouth. The freshness of the mint was a temporary relief, and he began to wonder whether another drink would fix him up. This sun was a lot hotter than he remembered, and he wondered how many days he'd last working on a farm like this.

Still thinking about the farmhand, he looked over at Joanna. 'Wait a tick,' he said as he walked out towards the machinery shed next to the homestead.

'Terry, I presume?' he said, guessing it was the young farmhand who had found Rose. 'Detective Nick Vada. I'd like to ask you a few questions about what you saw this morning.'

Looking over his shoulder and towards the homestead, Terry nervously leant his broom against the tyre of the giant tractor, which occupied most of the shed.

'Ah yeah, sure officer,' Terry said quietly.

'Call me Nick, mate. Give me a rundown of what happened this morning.'

'Sorry. Well, I usually check the pumps at 4am early before sunrise, but Pete asked me to fill up his and Mr Waterford's utes last night before they left for the day, so I was running late. I made my way down to check pump two and found her body there.' The young farmhand's eyes began to well up, and his bottom lip quivered. 'I've never seen a dead body before,' he said, as he looked downwards at the hot concrete.

'I know mate, it can be a shock. Is there anything else you saw that seemed suspicious, or out of place in the morning?' Nick thought to himself that although quite upset, Terry looked almost frightened, as he kept glancing toward the homestead.

'Nothing,' Terry said quietly.

'Look after yourself, mate,' he said, handing over his card with his information. 'Anything you think of, let me know.'

As he walked back to his car, he couldn't help but notice Russell Waterford standing on the front deck, looking out in their direction. With a quick wave, he jumped into his car and made his way back through the gates and into town.

Chapter Six

Heading back to the local police station, Nick saw Jack's highway patrol car parked out the front, alongside a dusty old farm ute. Parking next to Joanna, the two walked into the police station building.

'Matt and Claire Perry,' Jack said, introducing them to Rose Perry's parents.

Claire Perry looked like she had aged 50 years in a day. With puffy red eyes and tears streaming down her face, she almost yelled in Nick's direction.

'Please, tell me it isn't true, detective.'

'Come, take a seat, Mrs Perry. Joanna, can you fetch them a cup of tea?'

Once the Perrys had sat down at the table in the office, he confirmed the news to the now grieving parents.

'She was found this morning, Mr. and Mrs. Perry. We are extremely sorry for your loss.'

Matt Perry looked at Nick and Joanna and began to sob, as his body shook uncontrollably.

'My girl,' he cried. 'My Rosie.'

Joanna passed a box of tissues over the table. Nick thought she was doing a great job, guessing that she had never had to break the news of a death before.

'You better find out who did this, Nick,' Matt said in his direction, and he realised that the old farmer must have remembered him.

'We'll do our best, Mr. Perry. We won't stop until we find her killer.'

After helping the Perrys back to their car and setting a time to ask further questions, Joanna walked back into the station.

'That was rough,' she replied.

'You did great,' he said. His headache was slowly getting worse as the day progressed, and he knew he needed to get away. 'I'm going to take a break.'

Heading out of the station into the sunshine and jumping in his car, he leant over to the glove box of his police vehicle.

Scraping through the remnants of paperwork and tablets inside, he found what he was looking for, a small mini bar-sized bottle of rum. Downing the bottle in one go, he felt the alcohol burn his throat and run through his body, then felt his headache quickly easing.

He drove away from the station, and decided he should stop off and buy some more appropriate clothes for working after only bringing clothes for a quick trip and the wedding. Driving down the main street and past the impressive town hall building, he parked at a 45-degree angle in front of Revell's clothing shop. A large shop front with a small upstairs apartment at the back, it had floor to ceiling windows displaying slightly outdated dresses and menswear. It'll have to do for now, he thought.

Walking through the front door with the bell chiming, he smiled as he saw Jemma sitting at the front counter, browsing through a glossy fashion magazine.

'Busy day?'

'Third customer,' Jemma replied.

'I'm after some more work appropriate attire.'

'Yes, I heard the news. Terrible. Rose came in here from time to time to buy clothes.'

'News travels fast. How'd you find out?' he asked.

'You can thank your sister; she's the one who told me,' Jemma replied with a laugh.

'Let's hope she doesn't tell too many people; I've only just notified the Perrys.'

Jemma paused. 'I'm sorry, that must have been hard.'

'It's my job,' he shrugged.

After ten awkward minutes of choosing the correct colour business pants and three checked shirts, he asked for her opinion on a tie.

'A tie in Milford? A bit formal, don't you think?'

After wearing a tie every working day of his life as a detective, he agreed. 'Yep, let's scrap the tie. I'll just take these,' he said, passing over his credit card.

'It is really good to see you again, Nick. Let's try to catch up once all of this business is sorted.'

'You too Jem, definitely.'

As he walked out of the shop, he thought that maybe his trip home hadn't been all a waste.

*****

The sun began to set and he looked at his watch as he got into his car. He decided he'd better go and at least say hello to his dad and let him know he was in town. Making the same familiar drive he had made for years, he turned left off the main street and down towards the south end of town, towards the football oval.

Turning into Evans Street, he looked across at his grandmother Kath's house as he drove past. Her famous rose bushes were now dead, and the grass was knee high. With a 'To let' sign at the front of the property, he wondered if anyone had ever moved in since his grandmother had passed. Making his way towards the dead-end street with the tall gum trees of the river in the background, he swung his car right into the driveway of his family home.

A small 3-bedroom post war house sat before him. It had beige-coloured weatherboards, chipped, and cracked from the years of harsh sunlight and lack of care. The front lawn was shorter than his Nan's, but it still looked like his Dad didn't put much care into it.

Making his way through the front door, down the familiar long hallway, and out the rear screen door, he heard the sound of a wireless radio playing classic rock, coming from the back shed.

'Dad?' he called out.

'In here,' came a voice from inside the shed.

Walking across the back lawn, which was a light brown colour and very much dead, he saw a pair of legs hanging out from underneath an old Holden ute.

'Pass us the 10mm socket, would you mate?' Tim Vada said to his son, with his hand outstretched out from underneath the front bumper.

Through muscle memory, Nick walked over to the old dusty bench top and grabbed the 10mm socket from its spot in the toolbox.

'I feel like you've been working on this ute since I left,' he replied, passing the socket to the outstretched arm.

'Yeah, well, it's given me a lot more happiness than you have over the past few years. Let me clean up, mate, and I'll meet you inside,' he said, rolling out from underneath the vintage car and tapping the front bumper. 'They don't make them like they used to.'

Standing in front of him, his father Tim Vada had a slight hunch now, after years in the sheds as a shearer. Wearing a blue singlet with dark tanned skin, rough after years in the sun, he smiled at his son with a crooked smile.

'It's good to see you, mate,' he said with a sigh. 'Be good if you spent a bit more time here now and then.'

'Work comes first, Dad,' he replied, unsure of what to say at his father's change in demeanour. Had his dad ever wanted to see him before? Not usually.

'Well, after all your years of work, your family might not always be around.'

'I know, Dad,' he said, unsure of how to finish the conversation. He always felt awkward talking about emotions with his tough working man's father. 'I'll see you inside.'

He walked back across the dead lawn and through the screen door, subconsciously not looking into his parents' room. Since he was a kid, he always felt a cold chill whenever his Dad asked him to go into the room, and he always made sure never to look through the door opening, so the visions of blood-stained walls would not flash in his mind. He always wondered how his father could remain living in the house where his mother was murdered.

Making his way into the dining room in the middle of the house, he almost ran headfirst into his little sister Jess.

Tall and thin like him, Jess always seemed to keep in great shape. It was always a bugbear for Nick, considering she had never been involved in any sports. Short cropped brown hair and shining blue eyes like her Mum, Jess had heard many times from locals how much she looked like her, now she was all grown up.

'Didn't think I'd see you here,' Jess said with a smile.

'Well, looks like I'll be here for a while, so I thought I'd better make some effort.'

'Thank you. He's been doing it hard lately, Nick. His cancer has come back, although he won't admit it to anyone. Dr. Smith called me last week to let me know. The wedding is the only thing he's been looking forward to for the last few months.'

'Well, I'm here now,' was all he could think to say, eyeing his father's fridge, hoping there was beer in there. 'Jess, please don't tell anyone else about Rose Perry's murder. Jemma Revell asked me about it today.'

'I'm sorry. I was just so upset when Pete told me the news. I actually taught her at the high school. I needed to speak with someone.'

'You lot aren't talking about me, are you?' Tim replied, walking into the dining room.

'They're saying it was Matt Perry's daughter, Rose. Nick, is that right?'

'Yes, out at Warranilla, in the far east paddock by the river. I'll need to speak to Pete tomorrow morning if you can arrange that, Jess.'

'Yep, I will speak to him tonight. Stay for dinner Nick, I've made some roast pork and vegetables for Dad, there's plenty to go around.' He imagined his little sister in the big kitchen at Warranilla, preparing a meal for her father. It was all still a little weird to him and would take a while to get used to.

After dinner was cleaned up, and Jess had departed for the night, Nick sat on the front porch with his father, with the last remnants of heat for the day slowly dissipating into the cool, clear night. After finding that his dad did, in fact, have a well-stocked beer fridge, he sipped his third beer, and felt the stresses of the day leaving him.

Taking another long, deep swig of the cold beer, he turned to his father.

'So, what do you make of Pete Waterford, Dad?'

Tim looked ahead, and out into the moonlit night, with the only sound being the quiet buzz of the mosquito light hanging on the corner of the porch.

'It's all happened quite quickly, to be honest,' he finally replied. 'He's all over the place with harvests and sheep sales, so

I was surprised when Jess told me that they were going out for dinner for the first time.' He took a drink from his beer. 'That was only eight months ago, so they certainly haven't mucked around. Look, he certainly used to be a wild child, but he looks after Jess, and I don't have a bad word to say about him. He even got me an engine from one of his old farm cars that I can use for the ute.'

His Dad was easily bought, Nick thought to himself. But he knew after years in the sheds as a shearer, he could see through bullshit and wouldn't lie to him.

'He's making quite a name for himself out at Warranilla. As Russ gets older, he's taking over the place; made a couple of calls that haven't quite worked out, I hear,' Tim said cryptically.

Nick said nothing, thinking that Warranilla was a huge responsibility for someone in his early 30s.

'And how's Russell taken it?'

'You know Russ,' Tim said. 'He's had good years and bad year's out there like we all have.'

'Do you think they have anything to do with this girl on the property?'

'Doubt it. My guess would be her boyfriend. He's a rough lookin' young fella.'

Nick made a mental note to ask the Sarge about a boyfriend tomorrow morning.

'Hmm, we'll soon find out,' he said, draining the last bit of his bottle. The beer was beginning to make him feel tired, and he yawned loudly, as they sat still in the cool night air.

Tim broke the silence, 'Mate I know we've had our differences but if and when the big day comes, we need to be there for Jessie, I'm going through a bit and it's good to know you're around for the time being.'

Nick was once again surprised at his Dad's level of emotion, thinking that the cancer diagnosis must be getting to him.

'I know Dad, I'm not going anywhere,' he said, surprised at how emotional he felt. He knew his Dad had had a rough few years after retiring from the sheds, and sometimes struggled with money. I should try to help him out more, he thought, looking at his now ageing father.

'Right, well, I need to get to bed before I fall asleep in this chair. If I'm out here any longer, Jack might pop past, and then I'm stuck out here for the night!' Jack and Tim had had legendary drinking sessions out on the front porch, and Nick heard it all through his front bedroom window as he grew up.

Deciding to leave his car there and walk back to the motel to clear his head, Nick walked back down Evans Street. He looked up into the clear night sky, with memories flooding back of the parties of his youth, sneaking through windows and night swims in the river. Everything was within walking distance and there was never any trouble with weather, something very different, he thought, to the long-wet winter he had just endured in Sydney.

Nearing the motel back on the main highway, he made his way to the kerb to cross the road. Stepping onto the road, he instinctively jumped back, as he saw a white ute speeding past, with the side mirror almost hitting him. It was going way over the speed limit. Now sitting on the grass nature strip trying to process what had just happened, he tried to make out the licence plate speeding off in the distance, but only got two faint numbers.

As he continued down the highway towards the bus stop across from the old motel, he came across a young woman sitting on the bench.

'Are you okay?' he slurred, and realised he may have had one too many beers at his father's.

The young blonde girl looked up at him and had tears streaming down her face with what looked to be the beginning of a fresh black eye. 'I'm fine,' she whimpered quietly.

'Who did this to you?' he asked quickly, looking back down in the direction where the ute had almost just run him over.

'I'm not sure,' she said through sobs. 'I was walking home from the pub, and I was hit from behind,' she said, as her chest began to heave.

'Which way did they go?'

'I don't know. They knocked me to the ground.'

After getting her to calm down, he learned her name was Taylor Dowd, and she was a bartender at the Coachman's Inn. Nick, having never seen her there before, asked if she was local.

'Yeah, born and bred,' she said through sobs. 'Finished school last year.'

'You didn't know Rose Perry, did you?' he asked, wondering if this was the right time to be asking that type of question.

Taylor turned and looked at him, tears now beginning to stream down her face again. 'Yes, she was my best friend. We were about to go away to Uni together.'

Nick flinched at her reply, realising it was definitely the wrong time to ask the question.

'I'm sorry. C'mon, let's get you home.'

On slightly unsteady feet, he wrapped his arm around Taylor's waist and slowly walked down the end of the street, and then onwards to Wood Street, where she told him she lived.

'Nick Vada. You're the detective that was in the local paper a few months ago,' she said, looking thoughtfully at him through her good eye. He wondered if she had learned of him through the one article in the local paper his sister had sent him earlier in the year.

'Yes, that's me. Born and bred here as well,' he said, with a warm smile. 'I'm here to find Rose's killer and I promise you I will do my best.'

She opened her mouth to say something in reply and then stopped. He could tell she was formulating what to say next, but was disappointed when she said, 'Thank you so much. This is me here,' and she pointed at the front gate at the front of her home. 'Goodnight.'

As she walked through her front door into her small cottage, he couldn't help but think she was hiding something from him.

Chapter Seven

The next morning Nick woke after a restless night's sleep with dreams featuring crunching gravel, flashing headlights, and muffled voices, and with a headache even worse than the morning before. He rolled over, sat up and looked down at his softer than usual belly and wondered just how he would survive drinking this much each day. Popping another two Panadol tablets and drinking a glass of water, he slowly started to feel like himself again.

After a shower in the old bathroom with its faded green tiles and cracked mirror, he swept his hair to the side and dried off. Walking back into the bedroom, he put on his newly purchased pants and dress shirt with no tie, and considered heading to the front reception to call a taxi so he could head over and pick up his car.

Hearing a knock at the door, he made his way over, opening it slightly, and squinted due to the bright sunlight coming through the crack.

'Morning Detective,' said Joanna. 'Don't suppose you need a lift back to your car?'

'Yes, please,' he said, feeling slightly embarrassed that the young constable had caught him sleeping in.

After picking up his car from his father's house, he made his way back through the main street towards the local police station. As the sun rose higher into the sky, he couldn't help but miss the cooler mornings in the city. He hadn't felt heat like this in a long time. Promising himself he wouldn't drink today, he stopped by Joe's, the local bakery, and picked up a takeaway coffee. Taking a sip, he felt the caffeine hit his veins and start to slowly wash away some of the remnants of his latest hangover.

Pulling up at the station, he turned off his car, and felt the morning sun already heating the interior up to an uncomfortable temperature. Steeling himself for the day ahead, he stepped out into the bright sunlight and made his way into the station.

Sipping on his own black coffee at his desk, the Sergeant grinned as Nick and Joanna walked through the door.

'Bit seedy this morning, are we, detective?'

'Nothing a good cup of coffee won't fix,' Nick said, holding his large takeaway cup up in the air.

'Well, you won't find a good cup of coffee within 200 clicks of Milford, but the bakery is the best we've got.'

'Any news from the coroner?' Nick asked the Sarge.

'Jesus mate, it's a Sunday.' The Sarge replied. Nick had so much running through his mind that he forgot it was the weekend.

'She's been transported up to Edithvale, but it'll be a few days before we get any news. This isn't the big city.'

He swore to himself, knowing that in the city, the coroners worked seven days a week. Things moved a lot slower in the bush.

'Right, well, Joanna and I are going to chase down Pete Waterford for a chat. We will be back later today.'

'You'll have just missed him,' came Jack's voice from behind them.

Jack Thomson had just walked into the station and heard the end of their conversation. 'Saw him on a header on his way out of town. I'd say Russell has sent him off to the wheat harvest.'

'Surely not,' Nick said. 'We need to talk to him about a murder investigation.' He cursed under his breath at his sister and wondered what she had said to Pete.

'I'd say he'll be a few days at least, Nick,' said the Sarge. 'Perhaps you can head over to the Perry's and talk with her parents again.'

He didn't think he could solve the Pete Waterford problem right there and then, so decided heading to the Perry's was the best solution.

'Will do Sarge, Joanna, you can drive,' he said to the constable, hoping he was doing a better job today of hiding how bad his hangover was than the day before.

Heading out onto the highway he came in on, he looked across at the vast canola crops spanning each side of the highway, their yellow flowers flowing endlessly into the horizon.

'You never quite get used to the smell,' Joanna said, cutting through the silence.

'I don't mind it. Reminds me of home.'

'Why did you leave? If you don't mind me asking.'

'I felt like I outgrew the place. I needed a change and wanted to see the world. I got so far as Sydney. Haven't gone much further than there.'

'Do you miss it?'

'When I'm away, no. When I'm here, yes.'

'It's beautiful here, the wide-open spaces, the river. I just love it.'

'Why the move to here?'

'I grew up in Melbourne. My father was a drunk and abused me and my brother from when we were little. The day the police first took him away, I swore there and then that I would become a police officer,' she said, with a faraway look. 'And that it would be as far away from Melbourne as I could get.'

'Fair enough,' he replied in full understanding. A lot of his colleagues had past trauma, him included, and he knew that after his mother's murder, he would stop at nothing to prevent what happened to him from happening to another family.

Joanna turned in through the two rusted gates at the entrance of the farm. Noticing the left-hand side gate broken off its hinges, he stared out across the paddocks at some of the livestock. The sheep looked old and worn out, like they had lived a hard life, their use on the property potentially almost over. The Perry farm looked a lot like Milford the town, he thought to himself: past its glory days.

As they made their way down the driveway, he noticed an old ute the same as his Dad's, in the shed covered in dust, beside a rusted old Massey Ferguson tractor. He made a mental note to tell his Dad when he saw him next.

He stepped out of the car, swiped the flies off his face, and looked around. A work ute with no windscreen or doors sat beside the house, with a dog stretched out across the driver's seat, asleep. Opening one eye to assess the officers, it made the decision that they were no threat. He walked up to the front entrance of the property with Joanna by his side, notebook in hand.

'Hello again, Mr. and Mrs. Perry,' he said formally. 'I'm hoping we could sit and have a chat.' He pointed at the tables and chairs on their front deck with a smile.

Mr. and Mrs. Perry sat together on the front deck of their small farmhouse; and he observed the state of the house which looked to be in disrepair.

'Hi detective,' Sue Perry said, through swollen and puffy eyes. 'Would you like something to eat or drink?'

The thought of eating while trying to survive his current hangover made his stomach turn. But he was taught in his first year as a detective to never say no to the offer of food during home interviews.

'Yes, thanks Mrs. Perry.'

'Please call me Sue.' Sue made her way back through the broken screen door inside to fetch some drinks and food for them.

'I hope you've spoken to Daniel Matley, the little bastard,' Matt Perry said, through gritted teeth and puffy eyes.

'Daniel Matley? Rose's boyfriend, I presume?'

'Was soon to be ex-boyfriend, caught the little bastard stealing diesel from my machinery shed.'

He wrote down some notes in his notepad, underlining the words 'stolen fuel' before replying to Matt.

'Do you think he had anything to do with Rose's murder?'

'I wouldn't put it past him. I gave him the serve of his life after I caught him filling jerry cans of diesel last Tuesday. I also yelled at Rose to get rid of him,' Matt said, with tears starting to well up in his eyes.

'You could never have known what was going to happen,' Joanna said softly.

'If I had known, I would never have let her out of my sight,' Matt replied, as tears streamed down his face. 'My baby girl,' he cried as he tried his best to control himself. Joanna made her way over to the farmer and put her hand on his to console him.

'Is there anything we can do to help?' Sue asked, walking out of the broken screen door with a tray of tea and homemade scones.

'If you can think of anything out of the ordinary that Rose had said to you, or you'd seen, please make sure you let me know,' he said, as he bit into the old and dry scone which wasn't making his hangover any better.

'The only thing different in the past few months- beside her troubles with Daniel, was that she had been working as a bartender at the local football club for the last five rounds of the season. She was down there a lot, and I definitely noticed a change in her over the last few months,' Sue said.

Nick made a note on his pad and underlined the football club.

'We are going to do our best, Mr. and Mrs. Perry, to get to the bottom of this. If you can think of anything else, please let us know.'

'Thank you,' Matt replied, using an old stained handkerchief to wipe his face.

Nick and Joanna left the porch and made their way back to the police car. He looked out into the dry and dusty paddocks and wondered just what trouble Rose Perry had got herself into.

'What do you think?' Joanna asked as they made their way back towards town and through the canola crops again, as the rice silos stood foreboding in the distance.

'I think the Perrys look like they are struggling. We need to find them some answers. And I think we need to speak with this boyfriend, Daniel Matley.'

He also made a mental note to talk to Jack Thomson about the football club. If something was happening down there, Jack would know about it.

'Maybe she accused him of stealing the diesel. He snaps and kills her?' Joanna wondered out loud.

'Pretty over the top reaction to something as minor as some stolen diesel,' he said, knowing that some people have been killed for less. 'We'll know more when we talk to him.'

His phone's loud ringtone interrupted them. Showing an unknown number on the screen, he answered.

'Detective Sergeant Vada. Uh-huh, right, ok, understood.'

'That was the Edithvale coroner. He's finished Rose's autopsy. Looks like they do work on weekends.'

They made their way back to the police station, and Joanna excused herself to tend to a pile of paperwork that he himself remembered doing as a constable many years ago.

His phone rang again and he smiled. His sister Jess was calling him. 'Hi Jess, Everything ok?'

'Sorry to bother you, big brother. Dad's due in Edithvale this afternoon for a check-up, and I can't get away from the farm. Any chance you could drive him there?'

He once again had a vision of his little sister Jess, wearing a wide-brimmed straw hat watering Mrs. Waterford's camellia trees and cooking in the Warranilla kitchen.

He cut her off. 'Any reason why your fiancé is avoiding me?'

'Beats me. I didn't speak to him today. Now we've delayed the wedding, Russell has sent him back off for harvest. I'm not getting involved in this Nick; you and I both know Pete's not a killer.'

Nick wondered whether his sister was keeping something from him as well. Choosing not to press, he replied, 'Yeah, sure, why not? I need to make the drive down there, anyway.'

Kill two birds with one stone, he thought to himself, and it might be a good chance to get some more town gossip out of his stubborn old man.

After grabbing a bite to eat from the local fish and chip shop, in the hope it might quell his latest hangover, he picked up his Dad and turned out onto the southern highway, then sped up to a comfortable 110km/hr.

Making their way past the massive rice mill and train tracks that ran alongside the road on the outskirts of town, he remembered a time when most of the rice in the region that was milled here was trucked down to the ports, and sent off overseas to different countries. During his childhood he would sit out on the bonnet of his Dad's ute, watching the line-up of road train trucks tipping out their loads of rice, ready to be milled and packed off, ready for shipping.

'A shame what's happened to the mill,' Tim said, watching his eyes gazing over the large silos. 'No decent rain in the last four years, and now, even if we get it, the government seems to take the water away from us.'

He didn't know much about how water allocation worked, but he knew that via a complex series of water gates in the river that the government authorities could control how much water the farmers could use for their crops.

'Seems to me solar power is the new thing out here?' Nick asked, as they got past the mill and further out of town and noticed the massive rows of solar panels tilted towards the sun.

'Yeah, apparently, I don't know much about it. Plenty of Chinese money flowing through the town at the moment,' Tim said.

Nick wondered just what the Chinese had to do with solar farming in the region, but decided his Dad probably wasn't the best to ask.

'How are you feeling anyway, Dad?'

'Yeah, good days and bad. It's my back that causes me more dramas than my lungs.' With the years spent being hunched over shearing sheep, he knew that backs were the first thing to go on the men. 'Shearing is a young man's game,' his Dad always used to say.

His dad had been a pack-a-day smoker for as long as he could remember, and knew that the repercussions from those cigarettes were finally coming to fruition. Choosing to change the subject, he asked, 'How often do you go up to Edithvale?'

'Every month at the moment, usually drive myself, but as you saw, the ute needs a bit of work.'

'And any progress with your treatment?'

'Doctors,' he scoffed. 'Sometimes I'm not sure they know what they are on about. Billie would've cut through their bullshit.'

He was surprised to hear his Dad talk about his mother; she was rarely spoken about as he grew up.

'Did the police ever give you any ideas about who they looked at back then?' he asked, hoping for more information.

'They harassed the shit out of me, which I'm sure you remembered, mate, but once Jack got on the detective's case, it was pretty clear I didn't do it.'

'What about Jim Hooper?' he asked of the notorious serial killer.

Tim sat contemplatively, mulling over the question. 'I met him once, you know,' he said.

News that wasn't shocking, Nick thought to himself, knowing that the killer had been a shearer.

'He sheared up at the Turner's farm for a time, cunning as a snake he was mate, I knew when I met the bloke something wasn't right in him,' he said, and then elaborated further, 'I don't know if he had anything to do with your Mum's death mate, thought it would make the most sense. I don't think Milford was big enough back then for two killers, she didn't have any enemies.'

'Well, I'm going to poke around myself, Dad, and see if I can find out a bit more.'

'Be careful going down that road mate, nothing will bring her back,' his Dad said, ending the conservation, making the car silent once again.

Sitting in quiet contemplation, they made the rest of the 100km journey to Edithvale mostly in silence, his Dad's talkative mood stopping, as they made their way closer towards the river town. Popping up around the same time as Milford, Edithvale was around double the size, with farming and tourism in the river town being the mainstays. He had vague memories of his childhood making the drive with his Mum and his sister to go shopping and watch the paddle steamers slowly chug up and down the wide, fast-flowing river.

As he slowed at the 60km sign coming into the entrance of the town, he noticed a white ute accelerating in the opposite direction towards Milford. Trying to catch a glimpse of the driver as he sped past, he read the sign writing on the door, 'Waterford Grain.'

Pulling up at the doctor's clinic, his dad waved him off when Nick asked if he should join him. 'I'll be fine. Go and sort your police business,' Tim said.

He nodded and backed out of his park. Making the short drive around the block and to the back side of the hospital, he found the entrance to the Edithvale morgue relatively easily.

Stepping out of the air-conditioned car and into the heat of the day, his air was taken out of his lungs. He wondered if the stomach full of fish and chips with this hangover was a great idea after all, as the reflection off the glass doors of the morgue entrance shone in his eyes.

Opening the glass doors and walking back into the cool air of the office entrance, he noticed a girl sitting at a computer quietly typing away. Walking towards the counter to introduce himself, he couldn't help but stare. Bright green hair with a full arm of brightly coloured tattoos. He thought that she looked like she belonged in Sydney and not in Edithvale.

'Detective Sergeant Nick Vada,' he said, flashing his badge. 'Here to see the coroner.'

'Through those double doors and to the left,' she said, pointing behind herself, not looking up from the keyboard.

Walking into the cold white room under the light of four fluorescent bulbs, he found the coroner hunched over his desk, writing on a notepad, with a cigarette hanging from his mouth; the ash precariously ready to drop at any moment.

'No computers coroner?' he said, making the man jump slightly in his seat.

'Jesus, you scared the shit out of me,' replied the old coroner, looking up and flicking the ash off his cigarette into the ashtray beside his notepad.

'Paul McNaughton,' he said with an outstretched hand. With a shock of white hair on his head and black-rimmed glasses, Nick couldn't help but think of Albert Einstein when he looked at him.

'Detective Nick Vada,' he said, matching the aging coroner's firm handshake with his own. 'Pleasure to meet you.'

'Read all about your business up in Sydney mate, great work,' he replied, referring to Nick's turbulent year last year on his first major task force case.

'Thank you,' he replied quickly, not knowing how to take a compliment. 'What have you got for me?'

Sliding his chair back from under the desk and making his way over to the one stainless steel bench in the room, the coroner pulled back the white sheet covering Rose Perry's once beautiful face.

'Not a lot to go on,' he replied, the cigarette hanging out the side of his mouth. He wondered what the smoking rules were down here in the morgue, not that the coroner seemed to care.

'Stab wounds in the chest, piercing her pulmonary artery. She was dead the minute the knife entered her. It's caused massive internal damage; I would say the killer used a serrated knife of some sort. Perhaps a hunting knife?' he queried out loud. Nick thought back to Pete Waterford and the bandage around his hand.

'No signs of sexual assault?'

'No, nothing at all. No DNA under the fingernails, no hair fibres on the body. Whoever did this was careful or lucky.'

'She was certainly dragged while still alive, as there are some abrasions on the back of her legs and buttocks, but the only thing I can offer is that a small piece of her dress looks to be missing, which I've noted in autopsy notes. I'd say it is either still at the scene, or it is an item of interest you should be looking out for.'

Nick scratched at his chin and made a mental note to tell Joanna about the piece of dress.

'Although there is one thing you may find interesting,' he continued.

Handing over the autopsy report, Nick's eyes widened when he read the notes at the bottom.

'Fourteen weeks pregnant,' the coroner said, watching his reaction. 'Such a waste.'

Twenty years old and pregnant, just about to head off to university. He wondered what must have been running through Rose's mind in the days leading up to her murder.

'Sounds like she had a lot on her plate.'

Leaving the coroner's office, now with more questions running through his mind than answers, he made the short drive back around the block to the doctor's office.

'How's it looking?' he asked his Dad, as the older man gingerly got back into the car.

'Yeah, fine mate, I'm not dead yet,' he replied through loud coughs. Lighting up a cigarette and winding the window down, he looked for a reaction to smoking in his police car. Nick decided to let it go.

'Yeah well, if you keep that up it may be sooner rather than later.'

Chapter Eight

The next morning, sitting back in the Sergeant's office with Joanna leaning against a filing cabinet, Nick updated the Sergeant with the news of Rose's autopsy and that the young woman was pregnant.

'What do you think?' The Sergeant asked in his direction.

'So, maybe Daniel Matley found out Rose was pregnant. She wants to keep it. He flips out and kills her?' Joanna thought out loud.

'It's always usually the boyfriend, or someone known to the victim. We'll know more once we talk with him,' he replied.

Looking over at the Sergeant, he couldn't help but wonder why he would leave the city so late in his career for a posting out in the bush. Wife long gone, he was a bachelor in Milford and certainly not that eligible, Nick thought, considering his age.

'He works out at the steel supply joint on the highway, they've been working day and night with a new government contract they've picked up. I'd suggest you start there,' the Sergeant said, leaning back in his chair and closing his eyes.

'Big night last night?' Nick asked.

'Yeah, maybe a few too many down at the footy club.'

'What about Turner's transport?' Joanna asked in Nick's direction.

His thoughts once again turned back to the long cattle trucks ambling through town in the beating sun.

'I haven't forgotten about them. Once we speak with Matley, we will pay them a visit.'

The Sergeant popped an aspirin into a small glass of water on his desk. Slowly drinking it, he winced at the disgusting taste. As he finished it, he wiped his mouth and again leant back in his chair with eyes closed.

'Close my door on your way out.' Was all he could manage to say.

Nick and Joanna excused themselves from the Sergeant's nap and made their way out into the blazing sunshine toward the car. Now sweating through his new checked shirt, he turned the air conditioning on in the car to the lowest temperature it could manage in this heat and they headed back out towards the highway.

Crossing the bridge and looking down at the dark green river, Nick thought back to rope swings and floating down the old waterway with Jemma and his mates. The more time he spent here, he wondered what the true reason was for him wanting to get away so badly? Was it the murder of his mother? The fact that his Dad had slowly turned away from him? Or maybe it was as simple as a young man thinking he knew better?

Turning off the bitumen and onto a neat gravel drive, Nick marvelled at the size of the two sheds before him. Attached to the fence was a large grey sign which read 'Southern Engineering.'

He knew that his childhood friend Mick Perkins had been expanding his business, through the odd mention on the phone by Jess. What had started out as welding some farm gates and ute trays for mates looked like it had turned into quite an empire.

Walking out to the car was one of his oldest friends. With curly brown hair nearly over his eyes, Mick always looked like he was due for a haircut.

'Nick Vada! Thought I might have caught you at the pub! Heard you were at the pub already working on Milford's most eligible women?' Mick said with a smile and wink. 'And who might this be?' He smiled in Joanna's direction.

Nick saw the slightest sign of a blush from his young partner.

'Constable Joanna Gray,' replied Joanna. 'Pleasure to meet you.'

'Mick Perkins constable, the pleasure is mine,' he said, returning her bright smile.

'Mick, long time no see mate. Yes, I was at the pub and sorry I didn't bump into you. Just ran into Jemma, and caught up like old times.'

'The one that got away,' Mick said with a wink in his direction, still smiling from ear to ear.

'How can I help you two? I'm guessing you're here on official business, looking at those flash clothes you've got on?' Mick said, pointing at Nick's checked shirt and chinos.

He laughed to himself, thinking just how much more shit he would've got if he had worn the tie around town. Good advice from Jemma.

'I am sadly. Young Daniel Matley, working today?'

Mick's smile faded slightly. 'He's a silly bastard. I told him to take a week, a month, however long you need. But you know these young blokes,' he said, shaking his head. 'Money seems to be more important than anything else.'

Nick said nothing, wondering how someone who had just lost their partner could possibly work a few days later.

Walking through the middle of the shed, Mick's arms were pointing to different machines. 'Laser cutters from Romania, and a fifty-tonne crane,' he said as he pointed overhead to the large red crane on rails that slowly moved above them.

'Business must be booming,' Nick said.

'Busiest we've ever been, mate. The Chinese have begun building solar farms in the region. Apparently, Milford's global positioning in Australia is one of the most viable for solar energy. An absolute gold mine, they tell me. Some locals don't like it, but the amount of jobs I've created, not to mention money I've been able to put back into the town, should hopefully shut them up.'

He was happy to see his old friend thriving and busy. After he lost his wife to breast cancer in her late 20s, Nick had wondered back where his friend's life might take him.

'He's over here in shed B,' Mick said, and pointed to a figure grinding down steel beams which were sitting on sawhorses out in the blazing sun.

Nick and Joanna made their way slowly towards the figure, watching him methodically run the wire wheel on the angle grinder up and down the beams, removing residue. 'Cleaning them up before they get powder coated,' Mick said, reading the officers' inquisitive minds. 'Oi! Daniel!'

The figure switched his grinder off and flipped up his safety helmet. Daniel Matley was scrawny with short, cropped hair and a pock-marked face, and a southern cross tattoo on his arm shone through his sweat. 'Yeah?' he asked with a confused look on his face.

'Detective Sergeant Vada and Constable Joanna Gray,' Nick said in Matley's direction. 'Mr. Matley, hoping I could ask you a few questions?'

'Well, it's not like I can say no,' he replied. 'At least I'll get out of the sun for a bit.'

They made their way over into the air-conditioned lunchroom beside the sheds. Neat white tables and chairs were on each side of the room, and calendars of nude women lined the walls. A footy tipping competition which looked to be from a few years earlier had not been taken down.

'I'm sorry for your loss, Mr Matley. Can I ask your whereabouts on Friday night?' he asked, opening his notepad to a fresh page.

'Home at Mum and Dad's,' Matley replied quickly. Nick noticed that although the temperature was considerably colder in the lunchroom, Daniel was still sweating quite hard.

'And your Mum and Dad can vouch for your whereabouts?' Joanna said.

'Ahh no, they've been away for a month up at Darwin, but I was home all night. Watched the cricket, had a few beers, and went to bed. You're wasting your time,' he said with a shake of his head. 'I didn't kill her; I haven't even seen her for the last week.'

'We're not accusing you of anything, Daniel,' he said, hoping that using his first name might help establish a rapport. 'We just want to know a bit about your and Rose's relationship. Anything we should know?'

'Well, she was fuckin' pregnant, that's what you should know. And the bitch hadn't put out for months after I slept with that girl from Edithvale, so you tell me, detective, should you be talking to me or the father?'

Nick leant back in his chair. As he looked across the table, he wondered if he was staring into the eyes of Rose's killer.

'Yes, I knew that, Daniel. It was confirmed by the coroner. Any ideas about who the father might be?'

'Probably some footy player,' Daniel replied with a sigh, as the tension in the room slowly dissolved. 'She seemed to spend all her spare time down there with her friend Taylor and all those footy blokes.'

He underlined the football club again, remembering he needed to speak to Jack as soon as possible for further information.

'What was she doing at the club?' he asked, already knowing the answer.

'Bartending apparently,' he scoffed. 'But with the money she was making down there before she went off to university, she could've bought a car for herself instead of flogging mine all the time.'

'Okay, thank you Dan. I'd like you to pop into the station early next week and answer a few follow-up questions, if that's okay?'

'Fine by me,' he replied, as he began to stand up. 'Is that all? I've got work to do.'

'You're free to go,' Joanna said.

'You're talking to the wrong person,' he said over his shoulder as he walked back out into the blazing sunshine. Nick and Joanna stood up inside the air-conditioned lunchroom and stared at each other. Each with more questions than answers after the interview, they made their way back out through the hot sheds.

'Get anywhere?' Mick asked the two officers as they made their way out.

'He certainly doesn't seem too knocked around by it,' Nick said.

'No,' Mick replied, wiping grinder dust off his hand. 'He doesn't.'

'Heard anything in the sheds?' Joanna asked.

'Not these days, sadly. The boys treat me like the big boss these days. I don't get any gossip.' It made Nick wonder, after the death of his wife, just how many friends Mick had left in the dwindling town. 'Don't be a stranger Nick, we'll have to catch up for a beer soon.'

'Sure,' he replied, feeling sorry for his old friend.

Hopping back into the Landcruiser, Joanna was the first to speak. 'Known him for long?' she asked.

'Met in Primary School. The only Greek family in town, although not sure how many Perkins there are in Greece,' he said with a laugh. 'We were about the only two kids who didn't play footy. We were useless out there, mostly just sat in the stands and ate lollies and watched.'

'He's certainly done well for himself.'

'Very well. He's a hard worker. He was welding old farm equipment for pocket money as soon as he learnt. He's built from there.'

'Very impressive,' she replied. He wondered if the young constable had a crush and made a mental note to let his old friend know.

'So Matley knew about the pregnancy. We now know that, he readily admitted it,' he said. 'But he's claiming he is not the father.'

'Well, he knows if we think he's the father, he has a motive,' she replied.

'And no alibi.'

Driving back in on the southern highway towards town, Joanna dropped Nick off to his car at the police station with a wave.

As he got into his own car, his mind raced. He wasn't sure what direction the case was heading and decided to go for a drive and clear his head. Once again, crossing the bridge over the river, he looked out across the dark water, sparkling in the dying afternoon sun. Looks perfect for a swim, he thought to himself, as he indicated left, down towards the local caravan park.

A long white Volvo bus with Merlin's Coaches written on it was parked in tight and taking up most of the car park. Noticing three Chinese men in grey business suits looking out across the river, he watched them curiously. It was far too hot for suit jackets this time of the year, he thought, and also an odd time to be visiting Milford before the usual Christmas peak time for tourists.

After a refreshing swim in the river, he made his way back towards his motel room and wondered whether he should stop past the local fish and chip shop, or if he should attempt the pub again. His mind was made up for him as he opened his motel room door and picked up the small note that had been slipped underneath it.

'Dinner at 6, Coachman's Inn, J xx.' He read the note over twice with a smile on his face, thinking that it was his first date in a while.

After a quick shower and a change of clothes, he walked over to the pub in the dying light of the day. Utes slowly turned in out the front, as local workers and farmers stopped in for a quick beer on their way home.

Making his way through the main bar and into the bistro, he saw Jemma sitting at a small table, laughing along with Jack and Nell Thomson. He noticed her long slender legs showing underneath her light blue sundress. She really didn't age, he thought to himself, and hoped she thought the same of him, too.

'You lot live here?' he said, interrupting the three who were in deep conversation.

'Just breaking up the first date!' Jack Thomson said loudly, causing Jemma to blush.

'Cut it out, Jack,' he replied quickly. 'Just two old friends having dinner.'

'Mind if we join?' Nell asked.

'Of course,' Jemma replied, quickly looking at Nick.

Slightly disappointed, he made his way back to the main bar to order a round of drinks.

'Caught that killer yet?' asked one of the old bar flies perched up at the end of the table. 'Probably one of those Chinamen,' he said, pointing over to the back corner of the bistro.

Nick turned and looked over to the far corner to see the same three Chinese men from the caravan park, deep in conversation with Samantha Waterford. It was an odd place to see her, and he wondered if she'd ever set foot in this pub in her life.

'What did I miss?' he asked, walking back to the table with a round of drinks.

'I was just telling Jemma how much you two remind me of your Mum and Dad when they met,' Nell said.

'She was an amazing woman, mate,' Jack said.

He wasn't in the mood to talk about the past. Changing tack, he said 'Jack, mind if I have a minute?' and pointed over to an empty booth beside the main bar.

'Sure mate, we'll leave these two lovely ladies to order for us.' He winked at Nell and followed Nick over to the booth.

Sitting down in the old booth, he looked across at his father's oldest friend. Reliable and trustworthy; was the way his father had always described Jack.

'Official business, Jack,' he said, pulling his small notepad out of his back pocket. 'Hearing from a few people now, that Rose Perry was a popular member down at the local football club?'

'Brilliant netballer,' Jack said, sipping the froth off the top of his beer. 'Even better bartender. She's been playing for the Bears for a couple of years and bartending for the last few months; her and the bar girl that's usually here, Taylor,' Jack said, pointing in the direction of the bar. 'She worked the odd poker night down at the club rooms, but nothing untoward happens down there, mate, just blokes being blokes having a bit of fun. Even the Sarge attends and loses his money each month.'

Nick thought of the local football grounds and clubrooms he'd hung about as a kid. A gifted runner, the skill had never transferred onto the football field. 'A damn shame,' Jack had always said to him. He loved to run but couldn't kick or mark a ball for the life of him.

'She getting about with any footballers or anyone you know of? I spoke with her partner Daniel Matley today, and he seemed to believe she may have been cheating on him.' He decided to keep his cards close to his chest, mentally reminding himself to tell Joanna tomorrow to keep the pregnancy of Rose a secret for as long as they could.

'No one comes to mind,' Jack replied, scratching the stubble on his chin. 'She was a very friendly girl. Easy on the eye, God rest her soul, she was nice to everyone.'

He sipped his beer contemplatively, wondering if his old friend Jack was hiding something from him as well. He knew it wasn't the time or the place to push.

'What do you know about Turner's transport?'

'Turner's? Cattle carting mob from up north. They've got 14-15 trucks these days.' Nick wrote in his notepad as Jack continued. 'Milford's gotten smaller as they've got bigger, but there's big money in livestock these days, Nick. More money than grain, and I think they're getting involved in solar too.'

'Russell Waterford tells me he saw one of their trucks out speeding past his farm the night Rose was killed.'

Jack scoffed. 'The old bastard is always complaining to me about it. I'm only one man, Nick. They're all flying around the joint, half of them have pulled out their speed limiters, and who knows what they are taking to keep themselves up all day and night. There may have been one out that way that night, but I didn't see anyone.'

'Might be worth a drive out there then,' he said, closing his notepad. 'Let's see where our food's at.'

After an enjoyable dinner full of laughs and conversation, Nick and Jemma made their way back over to the booth near the main bar for a nightcap.

'So, how's your first few days been back in town?' Jemma said, with what looked to be another empty wine glass in her hand.

'Full of surprises. Another?' he asked, pointing at her glass. 'I feel like all there is to do in this town is drink.'

'Nothing better to do. Milford's not exactly the thriving metropolis it was when we were growing up, Nick.'

'Why did you stay when Dean left?'

'Mum was alone here, and I guess I just got too comfortable.'

'Have you ever thought of moving away?'

'Yes, of course, from time to time, but my Mum's getting older, and I have no one else.'

'I get that. It's how I feel sometimes in the city,' he said, surprised at how candid he was being. 'Work keeps me busy, though.'

'How is the case going?' she asked. 'It's okay if you don't want to talk about it.'

'It's going,' he said. 'I just feel like the answer is right in front of me and I can't see it.'

As the music changed on the jukebox, he saw that some of the younger crowd were up and dancing.

'I love this song,' she said with a smile. 'Shall we have a dance?'

It must have been the drink, he thought to himself when he answered, 'Why not?'

As he spent the next hour embarrassing himself on the dance floor and harassing Marty the publican for more and more elaborate shots, he once again felt a happiness that he hadn't had since his teen years back at home. The stress of the case falling away, they both stumbled out of the pub doors and into the moonlit night.

'Do you need me to walk you home?'

'With a killer on the loose, it may be a good idea,' she replied almost too quickly.

They made their way slowly towards Jemma's house above the shopfront, laughing and reminiscing with stories of friends and family. They got to the front door and before he could say, 'Goodnight.' Jemma turned and kissed him long and hard.

Electricity surged through his body and his mind returned to his teenage years with her. 'Mum's away at the moment. I think you should come in,' she said with a mischievous smile.

Chapter Nine

Nick's phone rang loudly on the bedside table.

He sat upright slowly, trying to get his bearings. Sunlight streamed through the curtains of his motel room, and he cursed himself for drinking too much yet again. Thinking back to the previous night, he smiled to himself, as the night slowly came back to him; a blur of laughter and heavy breathing.

'Hello?' he answered to the unknown caller.

'Good morning detective, need another lift?' replied Joanna.

'Hi constable, come and grab me from my motel. Busy day.'

'I'm on my way.'

After updating Joanna on his conversation with Jack the night previous, they made their way back to the local police station. He excused himself and went out to the rear courtyard for some fresh air, as the hot weather made him feel like the previous night's shots were going to come back up.

Sitting in the small courtyard with a coffee, he read through his notebook, trying to make connections that he just couldn't quite grasp yet.

'Bloody Taylor Dowd, can't believe we get that quality in town!' came a voice from the scaffolding running across the side of the neighbouring building. 'I don't play football, but I'm glad to be involved!'

His ears perked up, and looking over towards the direction of the voices, he noticed two young carpenters nailing off a fascia board at a precarious height, off old homemade scaffolding.

'Hi boys,' he said from down below. 'Mind if I ask you a few questions?'

Startled, the young tradesmen turned around to see the detective standing there.

'Uh, yeah, sure officer,' replied the oldest of the two.

'Detective,' he said, correcting him. He made his way down the side footpath of the police station and through the temporary fencing of the new home, stepping onto the scaffolding at the front of the house, feeling it move slightly from side to side, he felt like he was on a boat in the ocean.

'Detective Sergeant Nick Vada,' he said to them, flashing his badge.

'Hi detective, Matt Moore,' said the oldest of the two, and he pointed towards the younger carpenter. 'Jeremy Green.'

'What were you saying about the football club?'

'Nothing really. If my wife knew what we were up to, she'd bloody kill me.'

'I'm not concerned with talking to your wife, Mr Moore. Can you fill me in on what's happening down there?'

'It's nothing bad,' Jeremy replied. 'The monthly poker night down at the clubrooms has a couple of topless barmaids. No harm in it,' he said.

'And those barmaids' local?' Nick asked.

'Yeah, one of them was Rose Perry,' the younger carpenter spat out a little too quickly, with the elder scowling in his direction.

He thought of his chat with Jack the previous night and knew the old highway patrolman had been hiding that information from him. He assumed he probably just didn't want Nell to find out, but was frustrated he left a key detail out like that.

'And who organised these poker nights?' he asked, underlining the words in his notepad.

'Daniel Matley,' said Matt. 'The bloke's an entrepreneur and can play footy, that's for sure.'

He wondered why Matley had lied to him, and what else he may be hiding. He cursed himself for not asking Jack if Matt was a player down at the club.

'Any other locals?'

'Just that blonde bartender from the Coachman's,' said Jeremy. 'What a rack. Couldn't keep her hands off Dan the other night either.'

'Taylor Dowd?' he asked, wondering what the connection between her and Matley was.

'Yeah, that's her,' the young carpenter replied.

'Thanks for your time, gentleman,' he said.

Making his way back down off the scaffolding, he wondered what young Taylor Dowd and Rose had got themselves into. Walking back into the station, he called out to Joanna.

'Hey, Let's give Daniel Matley another visit.'

'Happy to get away from this paperwork,' she said, pushing the large pile away from herself.

After lunch and during the drive over, he updated Joanna on the news he had heard from the tradesmen. Making their way to Kleive Street on the east side of town, Joanna turned into a neat cottage-style home with light green trim and large satellite dishes up on the roof.

'Daniel Matley's parents' house,' she said.

They made their way up to the white screen door, knocking sharply, and heard, 'Come in, I'm in the lounge room.' Opening the door and walking down the main hallway, they found Daniel Matley sitting in his lounge room, with a beer in hand and the horse racing turned up loud.

'Can I help you?' Daniel asked.

'Just a couple more questions Daniel,' Nick said, still irritated that the young footballer had lied to him.

'Caught the killer yet? Rose's old man may kill me before you do.' He sipped from the beer can and put his cigarette out in the ashtray beside him. The smell of cigarette smoke was overpowering in the small room.

'Bit early for that, isn't it?' Joanna asked.

'Never too early, gorgeous.' Daniel said, winking at her, and holding his beer up.

'We are making progress,' he said, ignoring him. 'You never told us you played football for the Bears?'

'Well, you never asked,' Daniel replied. 'I'm a winger, coach reckons another pre-season and I'll be ready for..'

He cut him off. 'And organiser of the local poker nights?'

'Ah that,' he replied, as his confidence looked to be leaving him. 'Poker's not illegal.'

'No, it's not,' Joanna replied. 'A little demeaning to the women, though, isn't it?'

'They're adults. It's not my problem if they want to flash their tits for a bit of extra cash.'

'Your own girlfriend, though?' Nick replied.

'Well, she made more money than any of the other girls, so who am I to stop her?'

He found the lack of care for his recently deceased girlfriend disturbing. 'Who else was attending these poker nights?'

'Anyone and everyone: the footy team, Jack Thomson, Pete and Russell Waterford, even your own Sergeant, would make an appearance from time to time,' he said with a grin.

'And how close are you with Taylor Dowd?'

With a smile curling on his lips, Daniel replied, 'Close enough.'

Joanna's radio chirped. 'Milford 101, come in?'

'Here,' she replied, as she walked out of the room.

'You're welcome to come down and join the fun detective,' said Daniel.

'No thanks,' he said. 'I'll be keeping an eye on you, mate.'

'Look forward to it,' Daniel yelled at his back as Nick turned and walked back out of the hallway into the afternoon sun.

'I don't trust him,' Joanna said, as they climbed back into the Landcruiser, reading his mind. 'He gives me the creeps.'

Nick said nothing, as his mind wandered, and searched for a thread that seemed just in front of him.

Back at the station with her pile of paperwork looking to be growing, he left her alone and decided to go for a walk. Heading left out the gate of the police station, he slowly walked down the street, laying the case out in his mind.

He had 20-year-old Rose Perry from a nice family, a full life ahead of her and only weeks away from leaving for university, bartending topless at the local football club and brutally murdered. It didn't all quite add up. And just what did Daniel

Matley and Pete Waterford have to do with the crime? With Daniel, being the likely suspect, Nick still couldn't shake the feeling in the pit of his stomach that something wasn't right with the younger Waterford.

Subconsciously heading back towards the river, he found himself at the top of the riverbank near the caravan park once again. Massive gum trees swayed in the breeze, and he thought of simpler times when he, Jemma and Mick would ride their bikes here after school and swim until sunset, the only thing stopping them were the hungry mosquitoes.

'Detective?' came a soft voice from behind him.

Standing near the trunk of a dying gum tree was Taylor Dowd, with her black eye nowhere to be seen, he noticed that it was layered heavily with the foundation. She was absolutely beautiful; he thought to himself. Similar to Rose, she didn't look like she belonged in Milford. Her thin, tanned legs shone in the sunlight under her cutoff denim shorts.

'Hi Taylor.'

'I wanted to thank you for the other night. I'm sorry you found me like that.'

'No problems at all, just doing my job.'

Seeing that she was close to tears, he made his way closer to her, noting that her foundation was cracking in the heat of the day.

'Are you ok?'

'I'm in trouble Nick,' she began to sob. 'And I don't know who to turn to.'

'What's wrong?'

'I-uh found out something that I'm not supposed to know,' she said, tears now beginning to ruin her already cracked makeup. 'And I'm worried if I tell anyone he will hurt me.'

'Who will hurt you?' he asked.

Just before Taylor could answer, Nick heard another voice. 'Nick, Taylor, what are you guys doing down here?' Jack Thomson walked over, fishing rod in hand, with a big grin on his face.

'N-nothing,' Taylor said, wiping tears from her face. 'I have to go,' she said, turning around and walking back towards the caravan park.

'She alright?' Jack asked Nick.

'Yeah, I think so, just upset about Rose I guess,' he said, disappointed Jack had cut their conversation short. 'You catching anything?'

'Nothing at all, mate. Bloody waste of a day off,' Jack chuckled. 'Cod just aren't biting like they used to. It's mostly carp these days.'

'That's a shame Jack, we'll have to throw a rod in when all this blows over.'

Walking back to the police station and getting in his car, he thought to himself that the day had again presented more questions than answers. Who was threatening Taylor Dowd, and what did she do that had upset someone so badly that she would be attacked outside the pub?

Deciding to call it a day, he made his way back to his motel room with a six-pack in hand. Sitting down in the cheap plastic chairs out the front of his room, he took a long pull from the cold bottle of beer, which, worryingly, made his head feel a lot better with each sip. Grabbing his phone out of his pocket, he typed a text to Jemma.

'Dinner?' he asked. Three dots quickly popped up on his screen and then, *'Sorry, busy tonight, catch up tomorrow x.'* Oh well, he thought, might be the first early night since he turned up back in his hometown.

Chapter Ten

Getting up early for the first time in what felt like six months, Nick decided to go for a run. Putting on his sneakers from his car boot, he slowly and methodically stretched before his exercise, starting with his hamstrings and quads before working down and stretching out his calves. He remembered a time when he didn't even need to stretch, and knew that his best days were behind him.

Making his way along the cool pavement down the main street, and on down the southern end of town towards the river and caravan park, he noticed the tourist bus was still parked in the car park, and he wondered to himself why Samantha Waterford was talking with Chinese businessmen the other night.

The shrill ringtone of his phone cut through the still morning air. Slowing down to a walk and looking down, he saw that his sister was calling.

'Morning Nick, shall we catch up for dinner tonight? Warranilla at 7?'

'No worries Jess, I guess I'll see you then.'

'Great, bring a bottle of wine. Pete loves a re..'

'Pete back in town?' he said, cutting her off.

'Yeah, he got back last night. He's off in the east paddock, working on the fences. I told him to have a rest after the harvest, but you know him.'

'Jess, I need to ask him a few questions urgently. If you see him, please make sure he makes his way to the station.'

'All right, all right,' she now cut him off. 'I'll try to call him, although the range out there can be bad,' she said, before hanging up.

Why the reluctance to talk to him? What did Pete Waterford have to hide? The more he thought of the younger Waterford, the more his detective instincts seemed to come alive. He also wondered if maybe he was just being an overprotective big brother. He needed to speak with Pete Waterford and get to the bottom of this.

Back at the motel, he put his phone back on the charger. Walking over to his overnight bag, he pulled out the tattered and dog-eared manilla folder he'd found in Jack Thomson's shed years ago. Not letting it ever get too far out of his sight, he re-read through the homicide report of his mother, and chose to flick past the crime scene photos. Seeing the body of a murdered young woman in his hometown recently was enough for him.

Why did someone kill his mother on that fateful night in 1992? His mother was loved throughout the community, with friends far and wide. He wondered why anyone would want to hurt her.

Running the cold water to try to lower his body temperature after his morning run, he stood in the shower, letting the water run over him. Putting on jeans and a shirt, he made his way back out into the harsh sunlight and got into his car. Turning the air-conditioning fan once again to its maximum setting to cool down the inside of the car, he cursed as the seatbelt burnt his elbow as he clipped it in.

Parking at the front of the police station, he noticed a white Toyota Landcruiser ute parked nearby with 'Waterford Grain' sign written on his doors. He wondered if it was the same ute he'd seen speeding past him, coming into Edithvale.

Making his way through the front doors of the station and into the main office, he noticed the back of Pete Waterford sitting in the meeting room with a man in a suit sitting beside him.

'Just got here,' Joanna said, pointing at them. 'And looks like he's got a lawyer.'

Nick poured himself a black coffee and made his way into the interview room, wondering why Pete would need a lawyer with him.

'Before we start,' Pete said coolly. 'The lawyer here was Mum's idea. Nothing to do with me,' he said, pointing at the grey-haired, bespectacled lawyer.

'Detective Vada, Harley Campbell,' the lawyer said in his direction. 'I've advised my client not to answer any questions, but it's up to him.'

'Thankyou Mr. Campbell.'

'Pete, any reason why you left town after a woman's body was found on your property?' he said in Pete's direction.

'Harvest Nick, the seasons stop for no one,' Pete replied casually.

'Did you know the victim?'

'Rose? Yeah, sure I did,' Pete said. 'Bloody stunner, although don't tell your sister I said that. She tended the bar down at the local football club, saw her there all the time.'

With a knock on the interview room door, Joanna walked in and passed him a note, and silently made her way back out. Looking down, he tried to keep his emotions in check and hide his shock at the note which read: 'Anonymous tip came in, Waterford Grain ute, seen in the vicinity of Rose's murder scene around the time in question.'

He looked over at his future brother-in-law. With his collar pulled up and Waterford Grain trucker hat sitting high on top of his head, Nick still saw the young arrogant private school kid from his past.

'Did you have a relationship with Rose Perry?'

'Jesus Nick, I'm marrying your sister! Of course not. I'm like ten years older than her.'

He looked down at Pete's still bandaged hand.

Pete noticed him looking at his hand and instinctively lowered it under the desk.

'Hand still bothering you?' said Nick.

'This?' Pete replied, lifting it up back high for everyone to see. 'Pfft, it's nothing. Cut it on a fence.'

'Pete, would you be willing to submit DNA and fingerprints to help clear your name? We have received reports that a

Waterford Grain ute was sighted near the scene of the murder,' he said, looking for a reaction from him.

'Well no shit Sherlock, it is our farm, we have five of those utes.'

'Pete, in my professional opinion, I'd advise you against submitting your DNA,' the old lawyer said to him.

'Nah, fuck it, I've got nothing to hide,' Pete replied, surprising him.

Chapter Eleven

Nick watched Joanna package up samples of Pete's DNA and fingerprints, and send them off for analysis, and wondered to himself what the results of that testing would find.

'We have the murder on the Waterford's farm, and the phone tip about the Waterford ute being near the crime scene,' she said out loud, dragging him away from his thoughts.

'Not a lot to go on,' said the Sergeant.

'Yeah, and no other witnesses,' Nick said, looking over at the Sergeant sitting at his desk, wondering how the football club had a role in this, and remembering Jack talking of Rose Perry bartending there.

'Did you see Rose down at the football club Sarge?' he asked innocently.

Nick noticed the Sergeant go slightly red at the question. 'Yeah, sure,' he answered, voice level. 'She bartended down at the club a bit,' he finished.

'We've heard there might have been topless bartending going on?' Joanna asked, wanting to push.

'Nothing against the law there, guys,' the Sergeant replied, with his hands up. 'If I felt like it would've helped the case, I would've told you. Just a bit of harmless fun, I thought,' he said, clearly wanting to change the subject.

'I'm going to head out,' Nick said, hoping the Sergeant understood that they were just doing their job.

As the sun hit the highest point in the sky, he made his way back down the main street, hoping to grab some lunch from Joe's bakery.

Getting out of his car and into the blazing sun, he heard a voice yell out from behind him.

'Detective?'

He turned around to see young Terry, the farmhand from Warranilla, leaning nervously on the back of his work ute.

'Hi Terry,' Nick said. 'Call me Nick mate, you alright?'

'Thanks Nick,' Terry said, clearly feeling more comfortable now they were on a first name basis. 'Could we have a chat?'

'Of course, mate.'

Over the next fifteen minutes, sitting in the shade of the towering gum trees in the park, Terry told him about how he received a call from Pete Waterford in the middle of the night. Asking him to wash and fuel the work utes for the next morning.

'It was funny. I've never had to clean the utes before, and the lights in the wash bay were out. I said to Pete, I wasn't sure how good a job I could do in the middle of the night, but he didn't seem to care. He just said to get them ready for the next day.'

Nick wondered if there would be any evidence left in the wash bay on the farm. With mounting clues leading him in that direction, he wondered if it was time to request a search warrant.

'Thanks for letting me know, Terry,' he said, watching the weight come off the young farmhand's shoulders.

'Please don't let Mr Waterford know I spoke with you,' Terry said.

'Your secret's safe with me, mate.'

Nick made his way back toward his police car and wondered if Rose Perry had any connections to Pete Waterford.

'Nice of you to say goodbye the other night, Casanova,' Jemma said from behind him, as she leant on the bonnet of his car. She wore brief exercise shorts and a baggy t-shirt, and her long slender legs glistened in the sunlight. He thought she could've passed for a model in a magazine.

'Sorry about that. Can I make it up to you over lunch?' he asked.

After a quick lunch at the bakery with a smiling and laughing Jemma, he made his way past the wall of old local photos on his way to the counter to pay. A photo of his mother he had never seen before stopped him in his tracks.

Tall and thin with short, cropped hair, she stood smiling and holding a tennis trophy with 'Women's single winner 1981' emblazoned across the bottom. Standing beside her, with a smile on his face, and his arm around her waist was a younger, and much less grey, Russell Waterford. They looked too close to be friends, he thought to himself, making a mental note to ask Jack Thomson about their relationship when he saw them next.

*****

Nick made his way back to his motel as the sun began to set and the heat of the day began to dissipate. He put on his nicest shirt he had and his cleanest pair of pants. After checking the messages on his phone, he decided to leave it on the charger for the night. Walking out into the cooler night air, he walked back to the reception to fix up his bill and extend his time in town.

'Make it another week,' he said to the young clerk sitting at the counter. He wondered who else worked here, as the young guy was the only person he ever saw around.

'No worries detective,' replied the young clerk, swiping his card. 'Pleasure doing business. I'm surprised you're not driving a Waterford ute now that you're part of the family,' he said with a chuckle. 'Haven't seen one parked in my car park for a few weeks.'

'Why would a Waterford ute be parked here?'

'Meeting with grain buyers, buying new equipment. Seems like Pete or Russell Waterford's here once a month, at least for a night. Saves drink driving, I guess, and considering they own the place, why wouldn't you?' said the young motel clerk. That was news to Nick. What didn't the Waterfords own in this town?

Chapter Twelve

Making his way out onto the highway towards Warranilla once again, Nick couldn't shake the feeling that something just didn't feel right. He had threads exposed, dangling closely, but didn't know which one to follow. Knowing that he wasn't going to solve the case tonight, he tried to put it to the back of his mind and focus on the unpleasantness of dinner with Pete Waterford.

Driving down the long driveway of Warranilla, he once again marvelled at the beauty of the homestead. With the sun slowly creeping behind the horizon, the old homestead had a purple and orange haze over it and the massive gum trees around the home gently swayed in the breeze. It would be a beautiful place to live.

Pulling up and getting out of the car, he saw his little sister Jess chatting and laughing with Samantha Waterford, who had a wine glass in one hand and a hose in the other. Maybe she did do her own gardens, he thought to himself as he watched the Waterford matriarch, standing out in the evening sunset with a smile on her face.

Walking over to the ladies, he was relieved to feel the cool night air slowly beginning to set in. It had been a long day, and he was looking forward to getting this dinner over as quickly as possible.

'Nick! Welcome back,' Samantha Waterford said with open arms. 'Thank you for accepting the invitation. We are just so upset with all this business, holding off our Jess & Pete's big day.'

'Yes, well, I'm sure Mr. and Mrs. Perry don't really care about the wedding,' he said, bringing down the mood.

'Come on Nick, come and check out the back entertaining area,' his sister said with a scowl in his direction, trying to change the subject. 'Be nice,' she said, under her breath, locking her arm in his and walking up towards the front entrance across the fresh green lawns.

Walking down through the massive dining room, he once again marvelled at the size of the beautiful red gum dining table and the sixteen chairs. Continuing through the kitchen, they walked through saloon doors and into a lounge room similar in size to the dining area. Bi-fold doors ran across the rear of the house and with them all folded back, it gave the impression that the home was missing its back wall.

Stepping through the bi-folds onto the back deck, he looked up at the large white pergola roof with two massive fans the size of aeroplane props, spinning lazily overhead.

Standing over at a Weber barbecue with tongs in hand, Russell Waterford smiled in his direction. 'Spitfire propellers,' he said with a chuckle. Nick remembered his Dad telling him stories about Russell Waterford being in the army.

'Seventeen when I landed in Vietnam,' he said to Nick with some dramatic flair. 'I saw some things that would make your hair curl, young fella.'

'He was a spud peeler,' came a voice, walking through the bifold door opening. Pete stood sipping a cold beer without a care in the world, and with his hand just recently re-bandaged, Nick noticed. He continued, 'I probably saw more action than you did.' He remembered that the younger Waterford had also been an enlisted man for a period.

'Let's cut out the army talk,' Samantha Waterford said with a smile. 'Please Nick, take a seat.' They sat on the bench seats at the long whitewashed timber table. Sitting at the head of the table, Russell Waterford cracked a fresh bottle of beer and passed one over to his son. He looked in Nick's direction and said, 'Beer, mate?'

'Yes, please,' he said, hoping the case wouldn't come up over dinner.

After a delicious dinner of butterflied lamb, Greek salad, and homemade damper bread, Russell Waterford sat back in his seat and rubbed his stomach. 'Shit, I don't think I'll be able to eat for a week after all of this.'

'Thank you so much, Mrs Waterford. It was absolutely beautiful.'

'You're welcome Nick, you're family now,' she said with a warm smile. He noticed Pete bristle slightly at the word family.

Excusing himself from the table, Pete stood up and walked off toward the backyard in the direction of the machinery shed.

'Never switches off,' Jess sighed, taking a sip from her red wine.

'You know, Nick, I tell young Jessie all the time. Isn't she a spitting image of your mother?' Russell said, looking over in Jess's direction as she blushed.

'I get it all the time, actually,' she replied. 'Mostly from you,' she laughed in his direction.

Nick heard a smash and looked over in Samantha's direction. She had dropped her wine glass, causing red wine to go all over the floor. 'Oh, silly me,' she said. 'I'll go fetch a towel.'

Russell ignored his wife and continued, 'So Nick, any progress with the case?'

'We are pursuing all avenues, Russell; I'd like to think I'll have answers for everyone very soon.'

'It's a damn shame, so young. I'd be devastated if I lost Pete at that age.'

'Yes, well, finding a body on your property, under these circumstances Russell, I hope you understand why I had to bring Pete in for questioning.'

'Totally understand Nick,' Russell said. 'Samantha had the idea of the lawyer. Pete has a habit of putting his foot in his mouth. Didn't want him to incriminate himself unnecessarily.'

'Well, he didn't do it, so my big brother is wasting his time,' Jess said, cutting in. 'He was with me that night and again last night, so unless he's drugging me, he's not climbing out our window and murdering young women.'

He wondered why his little sister hadn't mentioned to him that Pete was with her on the nights in question.

'Maybe you should talk to your little sister more often,' she said.

'Yes, maybe I should,' he said, and then, hoping to change the subject, 'So, what's the story with solar in this region, Russell? Any plans for the future?'

Russell's face took a dark tone, and he wondered if he'd asked the wrong question.

'Those Chinese fuckers. They won't be getting an inch of my land,' Russell retorted. 'My family has been growing rice on this property for eighty years and I won't be the one to change that.'

Nick remembered Samantha Waterford in quiet conversation with the Chinese businessmen at the pub the previous night. What was that about then?

'They are coming in and buying up farms, and the solar energy is being bought back off the Government, so they're making an absolute fortune,' he said, continuing his rant, 'Little do they know when this current government is voted out in November, we will have full water allocation back and we will be producing more rice than any farm in the district.'

'And anyway, who can predict what will happen at the next election?' Samantha said in her husband's direction, as she walked back in with a tea towel.

'No need to predict it. I know they will win,' Russell said to Nick, and he wondered what ties Russell had with the incoming government.

'Fair enough,' he said, hoping not to be the cause of a Waterford family fight. Looking at his phone, he saw the time.

'I think I had better head off,' he said in Samantha and Jess's direction.

Jess stood up and grabbed a couple of plates off the table. 'I'll walk you to your car.'

'Been a pleasure, mate.' Russell Waterford stood up, stretching his arms up high and wide. 'Don't be a stranger.'

'Sounds good. Thanks again.'

Walking back through the kitchen and dining area in silence with his sister, he felt the beer beginning to go to his head.

'Might have had one too many.'

'You still right to drive?' she said, with a worried expression on her face.

'I'll be fine,' he replied, knowing the roads like the back of his hand. 'As long as Jack isn't out on the prowl.'

'Nick, I know all of this is crazy and you are just doing your job, but I promise you, Pete did not do this. He truly is a great guy and I'm sure when you get to know him better, you will agree.'

'I know Jess, I'm just looking at all avenues. I have to do my due diligence.'

He looked at his little sister with a smile. She really reminded him of his mother, he thought, thinking of the photo in the bakery.

'Jess, did you know Russell Waterford knew Mum back in the day?'

Jess rubbed her chin. 'Makes sense. He was around her age.'

'I saw a photo of them together, on the wall in the bakery today.'

'Oh yeah? I'll have to check it out when I'm there next.'

He felt uneasy. Unsure of what to make of it, he reached out and gave his sister a hug.

'Try to pop into Dad's tomorrow if you can, Nick. He hasn't stopped talking about you being back in town.'

'Will do.'

Hopping in his car and winding the windows down slightly to keep himself alert, he thought back to his first stint in the small country town of Kooleybuc, and some of the accidents he had seen due to drunk driving. He drove slower than usual, hoping not to arouse the local highway patrolman.

Chapter Thirteen

Nick awoke in a cold sweat in his motel room with the TV still on, and feeling the remnants of the night's beer swilling about in his head. Did Pete Waterford have anything to do with Rose Perry? And what else was Daniel Matley hiding from him? And why did he keep having recurring dreams of the night his mother was murdered?

He looked over towards the old case file sitting on the edge of the desk, with the reflection of the ancient TV casting it in a bright blue light. He felt like he had read through the notes a thousand times and almost knew them by heart.

The morning of February 6, 1992. Victim's husband calls 000 screaming for help to say his wife had been murdered. After sending a patrol car and ambulance to the scene, police discovered an unresponsive Billie Vada, in the rear master bedroom of the house.

Blood was splattered throughout the hallway from the killer leaving the property. Police noticed that it looked like there had been an altercation in the dining room. Scratch marks in the architrave of the dining-room door.

Officers also noted that the victim's two children were home during the incident and, through questioning separately, advised that they had slept through the night hearing nothing.

The killer looked to have pushed Billie down onto the bed, with one hand over her mouth to muffle her screams, and the other holding a knife.

Three stab wounds were noted on the body, one in the centre of her stomach and two closer to her heart. The local doctor at the time noted that wounds around the heart had caused massive blood loss.

Officers quickly closed off the house and the surrounding neighbourhood block, with a team of Edithvale patrol cars, sent up to assist in canvassing the streets to search for a culprit, and also question if they witnessed anything strange.

Detective Sergeant Jason Peters from Edithvale police was assigned as lead on the investigation, and quickly put it down to two likely suspects. Either Nick's father Tim. Or the man who had been terrorising the Murray region throughout the last few years.

Reading through the notes, he read of the process of trying to nail down his father as the number one suspect.

Life insurance?

Domestic assault gone wrong?

Infidelity?

Nick remembered how all his father's mates had said, how lucky he was to have found a catch like Billie. Cheating would be the last thing on his mind, Nick thought. The man loved work, hunting, and beer with his beloved Holden ute coming after that. But his number one priority above all else, was his wife Billie, and his kids. Although they had grown apart over time as he got older, from what he could remember of his mother and father together, it had been happy times.

The detective had noted size 11 boot prints leaving the scene. Later, confirming them as Red Wing boots by talking to local shop owners in town, he worked his way through the Milford and Edithvale shops, finding that most places at that time kept no records of a customer's name when purchasing shoes. A dead end.

The main priority for the detective, it seemed to him, was finding the murder weapon, hoping that fingerprints would nail down Tim Vada as his prime suspect. But after searching the neighbourhood far and wide, and even sending a team of police divers to scour the river, he came up with nothing.

After sending the children to stay with their grandmother, his father was taken to the station for questioning. Not being overly wealthy, he knew his father wouldn't have requested a lawyer, more through stubbornness than anything else.

The interview was conducted the morning of February 6, 1992, which Nick read in neat script writing in the report.

'Detective Jason Peters starting the interview at 8:01am.'

'Mr. Vada, can you please tell us your whereabouts last night?'

'Roo shooting detective. Go once a month, with Gary Jones out past Warranilla at the Waters farm,' Tim Vada said.

'And you were with Mr. Jones all night?'

'Yeah, we did a couple of runs through the rice fields looking for roos. There were none around so we set up a campfire, out in the back north paddock on the Waters' farm,' Tim said. 'Head out there now. Fire's probably still going,' he said confidently.

'And Mr. Jones can vouch for you?'

'Well, I guess. After we had a bite to eat, and a few beers we slept in our swags around the fire. He needed to be back in town early, so we packed up first thing and made our way back home. Why did it have to be Billie?' Why not me? How am I supposed to bring up the kids without her?'

'Is there anyone you could think of, Mr. Vada, who would want to hurt your wife?'

'No one, detective. Everyone loved her.'

'Is there anything else you can tell me that looked out of place?'

'Nothing,' Tim replied. 'Actually, there was one thing.'

The Sergeant replied. 'Go on.'

'Her wedding ring. It wasn't on her finger. She never took that bloody thing off, not even when she did the gardening,' Tim Vada. 'Maybe the killer took it?'

'Keep an eye out for it, Mr. Vada, and we will do the same. If you have any further questions, don't hesitate to come in for a chat.'

'Thanks Sergeant, please, I need you to find who did this,' said Tim Vada.

-Interview suspended 8:32am-

The last page of the report had held the biggest question for Nick, remembering the last few sentences. 'Victim's wedding ring was missing from her finger. Husband noted that she never took it off.'

He knew that his mother absolutely cherished that simple gold band with a large pear-shaped diamond, a family heirloom from Tim's mother, and some of his first memories were of his mother looking down at the ring, and smiling to herself.

Where was his mother's missing wedding ring? Surely her murder had not been over something so small. And why didn't he hear the killer enter the home on that night? Agreeing with the detective at the time, Nick also believed the killer to be someone his mother had known.

Jim Hooper's methods seemed to be a lot different to his mother's murder, with most reports being of savage beatings and extreme aggression. Nick didn't think the murders seemed connected, but over the years he had gathered as much information about the incarcerated serial killer that he could, borrowing case files, for research.

Reaching over to the bedside table and grabbing the remote, he turned the TV off and fell back into a restless sleep, dreaming of his mother and happier times.

Chapter Fourteen

She walked along the gravel footpath in the near darkness, with the dim light of the old floodlight in front of her being the only thing guiding her along. Holding a bunch of keys the size of a cricket ball, she cursed herself for agreeing to do the job.

Finally, under the bright light at the doors of the football club, she wrestled with the tangled keyring. There were keys of all shapes and sizes on the ring. After 20 awkward seconds, she found the one she was looking for, and shivered as the cool night air touched her skin.

Opening the doors to the clubhouse, she then started her job of stocking up the bar. She inhaled the familiar smell of beer tipped on carpet, just like at the Coachman's Hotel. She methodically stacking the bottles one by one on each shelf and turned the labels to the front as they went in. Her OCD was unable to let her do the job any other way.

Rose would've laughed at that, she thought sadly, her old friend being one of the few things on her mind over the past few days. Just who had killed her, and why? She knew she and Daniel had had some massive fights and she was fairly sure they had split up, considering how all over Rose? He was at the last poker night, but did he have the capability to be a murderer? She didn't think so.

She thought back to happier times with Rose, and how, after their first few weeks of bartending for the local football matches, Daniel had approached them and asked if they'd be interested in doing the poker nights, too. She and Rose thought, why not? More cash before university is always a good thing.

Attending their first ever poker night, the girls were shocked to see that the club had brought in topless barmaids from Edithvale. Rose almost left, but Taylor talked her into staying. And after serving some drinks, they got to talking to the pretty girls from out of town and soon realised just how much money they could make if they did it themselves.

She was the first to go topless in front of all the old local men and footballers and was surprised when Rose did too. They were both laughing at each other, knowing it was their last few months in this quiet little town, and they had no plans of ever coming back.

As Taylor finished stacking the bottles and cans in the bar fridge, a small noise made her jump. She spun around and looked out into the dark clubroom.

'Is anybody there?' she said.

She shivered as the bar fridge door stood ajar, realising that after her friend's murder and her attack, she really should not be down here alone. She wondered whether she should try to talk to that detective again about her fears.

Grabbing the keyring, she slowly turned the lights off in the old building. Realising how hungry she was, she hoped she could make the cut-off time for the kitchen at the pub. The chef had the hots for her and always made a great meal, if she smiled at him enough.

Walking out the clubroom door and turning back towards them, she put the old, rusty key into the lock, turned it and heard the click; satisfied of another job well done. As she began to make her way back up the driveway, she heard a voice cut through the darkness.

'I knew you'd be here.'

As the figure walked slowly into the light, she felt a cold chill run down her spine as she saw the long, sharp hunting knife in his left hand. She knew she had made a few wrong decisions, but surely he wouldn't take things this far?

She held both hands up in surrender. 'Please, I told you, I won't say anything.'

'That's not a risk I'm willing to take,' said the figure, dressed in black.

She realised her only chance was to make a run for it. Turning and trying her best to run in her sandals, she made it almost as far as the heritage grandstand.

The black figure caught her with ease, and pushed her with full force in the back, causing her to land hard on the cold ground, knocking the wind out of her.

He turned her over and quickly straddled her, trying his best to hold her arms down, as she scratched and kicked as hard as she could.

'Please, don't.'

With a swift driving motion, the figure stabbed her hard in the chest. The sound of blood gurgled as the knife punctured her lungs. Stabbing down again and again, the killer yelled, 'That'll shut you up!'

Taylor Dowd's last thoughts were of her best friend, Rose Perry, now knowing exactly who had killed her.

Chapter Fifteen

Nick's phone ringtone woke him up. Shielding his eyes from the sunlight blinding him through his curtains, he rolled over and answered the call, 'Detective Vada, speaking?'

'Nick, it's Jack. There has been another murder.' Nick sat bolt upright and rubbed his eyes.

'Where are you, Jack?'

'I'm down by the football club rooms. I was just opening up to clean up... and I found her,' Jack said in a strained voice.

'Who Jack?'

'Taylor Dowd,' he said, as his voice began to crack.

He couldn't believe what he was hearing. Two women murdered in the space of a few days. He had to get to the bottom of this. And fast.

'Stay where you are. I'm on my way.'

Quickly showering and dressing, he called the Sergeant and reported the news he had heard from Jack. The Sergeant let him know that he would call Edithvale Crime Scene Services and get them to head out there. Making his next call to his partner, he said, 'Joanna it's Nick, come past the motel and pick me up now.' Minutes later, he saw the white Milford police Landcruiser pull into the motel carpark.

'I was just heading in to see if any DNA results had come through,' Joanna said.

'What's wrong?' she asked Nick, noticing the stricken look on his face.

'The local football club. There's been another murder.'

Her mouth slowly opened. 'Shit, what the hell is happening?'

As they sped through the main street and towards the football clubrooms, Nick's mind raced, wondering who could possibly be killing women in his hometown. He was cursing himself for not catching up with the young bartender and not continuing their conversation down by the riverbank.

Joanna indicated at the small bridge and pulled into the entrance of the football oval.

The only other car at the clubhouse was Jack's white highway patrol car, parked under the shade of a gum tree. Joanna made her way in next to it, pulling the Landcruiser up to a stop.

Nick got out and walked over toward the clubrooms, wondering what he may be walking into.

'Nick, over here!' Jack called out from underneath the grandstand.

Walking towards the stands and thinking of the clubhouse, he made a mental note to ask his Dad if he attended the local poker nights; it would be good to get another opinion, he thought.

Beside the upright columns of the grandstand lay Taylor Dowd with a large blood stain across her chest; her eyes staring blankly up at the underside of the structure.

Jack stood quietly beside the body. 'I was just opening the clubhouse and saw her feet sticking out from under the grandstand. Sometimes I'll find the odd drunk down here and thought I'd come check it out.'

Jack's face was grey, and he wondered if this was the first dead body he had ever seen.

'Thanks for calling me so quickly Jack. Edithvale has a team on their way and I'll get Bruce down here, and we'll start having a look around. Could you grab some police tape from your car and secure the scene?' He thought giving Jack a job to do might take his mind off what he'd just seen. It was a bit more confronting than pulling over farmers for speeding tickets.

He knelt down beside the column of the grandstand and stared at Taylor Dowd's body. Black eye still fresh on her face, he wondered if the same man who had attacked her, and then threatened her, had also been her killer?

'She was a bartender at the Coachman's, wasn't she?' Joanna asked, cutting through his thoughts.

'Yes apparently. I came across her the other night and walked her home, actually. She'd been attacked, she told me.'

'Information you thought to keep to yourself?' she replied, shocked.

'She actually spoke to me again the other day,' he said, looking down at her body. 'She said someone was threatening her.'

'Well, she certainly put up a good fight,' Joanna said, pointing at the scratch marks on her arms and legs. 'Whoever we are looking for will probably look like they've been in the fight of their life.'

He turned in the direction of the noise from a white Volkswagen van, making its way slowly down the driveway. He had had a mixed relationship with Crime Scene Services in Sydney, with some of them being the best people he had ever worked with, and some being absolutely useless, missing vital clues that he himself had picked up instead in their wake.

Walking over to the van, he saw the passenger side door opening. Out popped a short young woman of Indian descent, with coffee-coloured skin. She had light freckles spread across her small button nose, and beautiful, shining, dark brown eyes. She walked over in their direction and he was taken aback by just how beautiful she was.

'Good morning, I'm Senior Constable Bec Ranijan, and this is Constable Michael Smith,' she said, pointing over her shoulder at the younger man who had been driving the van.

Nick could see that the young male constable was transfixed on a horse race on his phone screen. He had known many other colleagues in his time on the force that were obsessive gamblers. He couldn't, for the life of him, find any interest in it.

Tearing his eyes away from the screen, the constable walked over and held his hand out in Nick's direction. 'Nice to meet you,' he said. Tall like a beanpole with straw-coloured hair, the young Crime Scene officer towered over them both and Nick wondered whether he played basketball.

'And before you ask: yes, I play basketball,' Michael added with a wry smile on his face.

'Beat me to the punch,' Nick said with a smile. 'Detective Sergeant Nick Vada, and this is Constable Joanna Gray, and Senior Constable Jack Thomson,' he said, formally introducing the trio.

'What do we have?' Bec asked, as the group walked towards Taylor's body.

'Taylor Dowd, 19 years old, bartender at the local pub,' he said in Bec's direction.

'Any connection with your first victim?' Michael asked.

'Best friends,' Joanna said.

Nick and Joanna watched as the duo methodically started creating a perimeter with blue and white crime scene services tape, and setting up a small gazebo with a white camping table underneath it. Bec set out all the camera gear and evidence bags with precision.

Watching the two work, he was quietly impressed at the way they worked together; while Michael began to take photos with a black digital camera, Bec slipped on a pair of white medical gloves and began to check through Taylor's clothing for any clues.

Hearing it coming down the road before seeing it, Nick looked over at the black Ford panel van of the local doctor Bruce Smith, coming slowly over the small bridge at the entrance of the oval. Nick waved him over towards the police tape and grandstand and Bruce Smith got out of the car and made his way over to the body.

'Jesus, not again,' he said, more to himself than to them.

The elderly doctor walked under the gazebo and introduced himself to the Edithvale crime scene team.

'Bruce Smith,' he said, shaking hands with the duo.

'Good morning doctor, Bec Ranijan and Michael Smith,' she said, pointing over again in Michael's direction. 'Thank you for your help with the Perry crime scene.'

'You're very welcome. May I?'

'Of course,' Bec replied.

The doctor and Bec meticulously worked their way over the body, checking the wounds and also checking her clothing and pockets, occasionally murmuring things in agreement with each other. He couldn't help but stare at the younger crime scene officer. From what he could tell, she had absolutely no makeup on and her skin was absolutely flawless. She looked like a famous Indian movie star, and he felt like he recognised her from somewhere. After seeing how beautiful Taylor had been, and Jemma and now Bec, he wondered just what was in the water in these country towns. It seemed like all the women here were absolutely beautiful. Snapping himself back to the present, he looked expectantly in their direction.

'What can you tell me, doc?'

Poking gently underneath the young woman's side with the end of his pen, the doctor's brow furrowed.

'Multiple stab wounds obviously, similar to Rose, and defensive wounds,' he said, pointing at the deep scratch marks across her forearms.

'I'd say she's been dead for around eight hours. Lividity looks to be nearly set in,' he said, noting the discolouration of skin on her lower back.

'Right, so that's around 10am last night,' Joanna said from beside Nick. 'I wonder if there were any functions on at the club last night?'

'Nothing was on,' Jack replied, walking back within earshot of their conversation. 'I spoke with Taylor yesterday afternoon about giving the bar a clean out before Thursday's poker night. I guess I'm the reason she's here,' Jack said, with his eyes looking down at the gravel.

'It's not your fault Jack, it could've happened at any time,' Nick said. 'Why don't you head back to the station and call it a day?' he thought his old friend had seen better days.

Bec stood up from the body, removed her gloves in a swift movement, and wiped beads of sweat off her brow.

'God, it's hot here,' she said, walking over to Nick.

'You never quite get used to it.'

'Where are you from originally?' she asked.

'I'm actually a local, born and bred here.'

He thought he detected a slight shift in body language at that comment as the young officer smiled eagerly in his direction. He wished these types of women were in the city.

'Oh wow, most officers I meet in Edithvale and around are transports, all trying to get their country time up before they move into the city postings.'

'I'm one of them,' he said, as he explained coming home for his sister's wedding and being thrust into the investigation. As they stood away from the group under the shade of the grandstand, he updated Bec on the Perry murder and some of his thoughts around the case, filling her in on his suspicions about Pete Waterford.

After directing Joanna and Michael to begin searching around the grandstand to see if they could find anything, Nick and Bec walked around the far side of the clubrooms in search of clues. Looking thoughtfully in his direction, Bec piped up.

'I can certainly see where your train of thought is heading, but two murders in a town like this are pretty much unheard of. We haven't had a murder in the region in five years. It doesn't seem like something a farmer would be doing just out of the blue. Where is the motive? And why hasn't he done this before?'

He listened, enjoying being able to bounce ideas off a person who was fresh to the case. He wondered whether he was honing in too hard on Pete, but couldn't shake his gut feelings about the young farmer.

He remembered back to his first year as a detective. When he was investigating the case of a murdered teenager, he sat and listened through interviews with all the family members and couldn't shake the feeling that the quietest of the bunch, the uncle, had something to do with it. He pushed his superiors harder and harder until he got the opportunity to interview the uncle again, and surprisingly, through a different line of questioning, had him confess to killing the young boy accidentally, and then try to dispose of the body. After that case, he always tried his best to follow his gut feelings.

After searching around the back of the clubrooms and around the fencing that skirted the oval, Bec and Nick began to walk back towards the grandstand in Joanna and Michael's direction.

Looking out in Joanna's direction, he heard her excitedly shout to him. 'Nick, over here!'

He raised his eyebrows in Bec's direction, and the two made their way over to them. Standing in the long dry grass, Joanna and Michael looked down at something in front of them. Sitting in the weeds beside the bridge at the entrance of the football ground was a long serrated hunting knife, bloodstained, with the light grey blade glistening in the morning sun.

'Bag it,' he said to Joanna. 'Hopefully we can get some prints or DNA.'

Looking over the long hunting knife in the clear evidence bag Joanna held, Bec shook her head.

'Not a nice way to go,' she said sadly.

Putting his cigarette out and flicking it onto the gravel, Bruce said, 'Looks to be the murder weapon. Thickness of the blade matches her stab wound.'

'I agree,' Bec added.

'Can you guys help me lift her?' Bruce asked in Bec and Michael's direction.

'Of course.'

As Nick watched them help the doctor lift the body into the body bag, he noticed something underneath her body, between her shoulder blades.

'Wait,' he said.

Leaning in underneath Taylor's body, he pulled out a blood-soaked rigging glove used for farm fencing.

'Looks like the killer was in a hurry,' he said, passing the glove to Bec and watching her seal it in another evidence bag.

'Hopefully we can get some DNA from this too,' she said.

Nick and Joanna helped Bruce load the body into the back of the black Ford panel van. Nick tried to piece together a connection between what had happened to the two murdered women. Feeling like the answer was within his reach and at the same time far away.

He watched as Bec and Michael began to pack away the gear they had set up, and helped Michael with the gazebo. They sweated and swore as they awkwardly tried to get it back in the tiny bag.

'Bastards of things, these are,' Michael said, swearing at the black bag as it sat on the hot gravel.

'Nearly as bad as a tent,' Nick said with a laugh.

As Michael began to load the back of the van with the gazebo, Bec finished loading the camera gear neatly into clear plastic containers and made her way over in Nick's direction.

'We'll get all of this evidence logged and as soon as we hear anything, you'll be the first to know,' she said.

'Thank you,' he replied.

'No worries at all.'

While Michael sat in the white police van engrossed in his iPhone screen watching the next horse race at Flemington, Joanna made her way over and thanked Bec for her help during the day before, she then headed back over and started the police Landcruiser up. Standing the now beaming sunlight, Nick felt a single bead of sweat running down his back and felt unspoken words between the two officers.

'You married Nick?' Bec asked.

'Never. Had a couple of partners but it hasn't stuck. You?'

'Nope, not many eligible bachelors in Edithvale,' she said with a laugh.

He was out of practice, but he felt like the younger officer was flirting with him. Was he that out of touch? He hadn't even tried to get back in the dating pool since his last break up, but back in his youth, he had confidence when talking to women. As he got older, and a little bit softer around the middle, he definitely felt like it had ebbed, and it felt like the job was his life. But after seeing Jemma again and now having Bec seem to show interest, he felt like he was spoilt for choice.

'Well, if you're ever in Edithvale, give me a call,' she continued, handing over her police card. 'I'd love a drink.'

Ok, so that was definitely flirting. He laughed to himself.

'Of course, I'd love to,' he replied. Was that too keen? He still wasn't sure where his emotions were with Jemma. It had been so long, but was she interested in him seriously?

He waved the Crime Scene Services van off and walked over to the police Landcruiser, where Joanna was sitting in the driver's side with a wide smile.

'Ok, so she was definitely into you,' she said with a laugh.

'You think?'

'Couldn't have been more obvious. She couldn't keep her eyes off you.'

Heading back towards the station, he asked Joanna to drop him off back out the front of his motel so he could get his own car. Head still thumping from too much beer at dinner the night before, he walked in and reached over onto his bedside table and popped two more Panadols for his headache. I'm going to need a month's supply of them, he thought to himself as he cupped his hands under the tap in the bathroom and swallowed down the small tablets.

Hearing his phone ring again, he walked over to the stained wooden table against the wall of his motel room. Unplugging his phone out of the charger, he saw Mark Johnson's name on the screen. Shit, he swore under his breath. Another murder in his hometown and the Chief Inspector would think this case was getting away from him.

'Another murder Nick?' The Chief answered, cutting straight to the point.

'Looks like it, Chief, best friend of the first victim.'

'Shit. I've got Channel Seven and Channel Four on our media relations team's ass about the Perry murder, and the minute this news comes out, there is going to be a small army of reporters and camera crews heading to Milford. Nick, I'm doing my best to hold them off, but I need some progress mate.'

'Thank you. I have some avenues I'm running down,' Nick responded, unsure of what direction he needed to go next.

'Good, do you need reinforcements?' the Chief asked.

'No, I'm fine Chief, it's under control.'

'No worries, I'll let you get back to it then.' The Chief hung up before Nick could get another word in.

He rubbed his temples and worried about what his next move might be. He knew with the media descending on the small town, the circus would follow: brown nosers, true crime buffs, and private investigators all looking for the next Jim Hooper.

Getting in his car and pressing the elaborate silver buttons on the dash to get the coldest setting possible, he pulled up at the bakery and ordered himself and Joanna a takeaway coffee. As the coffee machine hissed in the background, he once again found himself walking over to the local photo wall and looking at the photo of his mother. He had never heard his Dad talk about her playing tennis. Looking at the size of the trophy, she must have been handy on the tennis court.

Moving in closer to the photo, he could just make out the shine of his mother's wedding ring on her hand holding the trophy. Moving back and looking at the rest of the group in the photo, the only other person he recognised was Russell Waterford, who had his arm wrapped around his mum's waist, smiling widely.

'Coffee's ready, Nick.' The shop attendant yelled out to him.

As he began to turn and grab the cups, he noticed something he hadn't seen before on the notice board. In small, neat capital letters above the photo, written in red ink was one word: LIAR.

He looked at the word, wondering who had written it and what its meaning could be? Why would anyone call his mother a liar? His phone rang, breaking his trance.

'Detective Vada.'

'Nick, it's Joanna. Meet me at the station.'

'On my way.'

Passing a ten-dollar note over to the shop attendant, he pointed over towards the photo wall. 'Who put those photos up?'

'Probably Joe back in the day, beats me,' the girl said, shrugging her shoulders.

He knew his father had known Joe as he was growing up, but the elderly owner had passed many years earlier and then a young couple took over the bakery.

'Thanks,' he said, grabbing the two hot takeaway cups of coffee.

Pulling up at the station, Nick walked through the front doors with two coffee cups in hand.

'Thank you,' Joanna said, raising the cup to her nose and smelling the bitter beans. 'Much needed after the last few days.'

'It's alright, I didn't want one,' Jack Thomson said from behind him, winking.

'Sorry Jack, I wasn't sure you'd be back in the station today,' he said, remembering the colour of the old highway patrolman's face after seeing Taylor's body.

'All good Nick, I think I'll stay away from any murders and stick to the highways,' he said, walking towards the front doors. 'You guys need anything, just let me know.'

'Will do,' he said to the back of Jack's head.

'Actually Jack,' Nick said and followed him towards the front door, out of earshot of Joanna. 'Mind if we have a quick word?'

'Of course, mate,' Jack said.

Standing in front of the police station, Nick asked Jack the question that had been bugging him for a few days now.

'Were my Mum and Russell Waterford an item back in the day?' he asked, already guessing the answer.

'Russ Waterford? Not a chance, mate. He was a few years older than your Mum and Dad and me. He married Samantha

Anderson young,' Jack said, referring to Mrs. Waterford by her maiden name.

'I saw a photo at the bakery of them at the tennis club.'

'Oh yeah? Your Mum was a gun with the racket. Old Russ was a tennis coach down there. I reckon he may have coached her for a few years back then,' Jack said, brow furrowing, trying to remember any more details.

'Thanks Jack.' Nick began to make his way back into the station. 'Catch up for a beer with Dad sometime soon, would you? The old fella's getting lonely.'

'Of course,' Jack said, walking over to his highway patrol car. 'Talk to you later.'

Walking back into the station, the Sergeant called Nick into his office, 'You too, constable,' he said, pointing at Joanna.

Taking a seat in the leather chair with Joanna leaning against the filing cabinet, the Sergeant opened a manilla folder on his desk in front of him.

'DNA results from Pete Waterford,' he said, reading through the report out loud.

He sat up straighter in his chair, hoping for good news.

'Checked against defensive wounds on Rose's arm and also against a single hair fibre, cut from under her fingernail. We report that the DNA we received from your office is not a match,' the Sergeant read out loud.

'Not a match?'

'Nope,' the Sergeant sighed. 'I would say that conclusively rules out Pete Waterford as the killer of Rose Perry.'

His mind raced. Unable to shake his hunch on Pete Waterford, he decided to press.

'Test the DNA and prints against the knife found at Taylor Dowd's murder scene,' he said quickly. 'Then I will cross him off my list.'

The Sergeant looked over at Nick with an annoyed glare. Joanna was first to speak, detecting the tension in the room.

'I'll send through the paperwork,' Joanna said, walking back towards her desk.

'Keep your options open detective, this one may be a little too close to home,' the Sergeant said sternly.

'Just let me know when you have the results from the DNA,' he said, as he got up and walked from the room.

Chapter Sixteen

Walking over to Joanna's desk, Nick watched her email through the relevant documents.

'Joanna, let's get out of here.'

Getting in the police car, Joanna asked what the next move would be. 'Turner's Transport,' he replied. 'We've heard about these truckies enough. I think we should at least check it out.'

'Good idea,' she replied, as she started up the car.

Making their way out towards the large white sheds in the distance, he asked Joanna if she had heard anything about the local drivers.

'Nothing of significance. Me and the Sarge have broken up a couple of fights between drivers at the pub. And I know Jack has done a couple of their trucks for speeding,'

'Nothing else?'

'Only rumours, we've heard that they may have something to do with the supply of drugs in the region; a couple of their younger drivers we know have been caught in Edithvale with various things, and they've got a couple of bad eggs working for them, I know that.

He remembered the amount of trouble he had with a transport company in the city back in his first few years of policing. They had an affiliation with a bikie club and had caused quite a few problems for him and his station at the time.

'Ok, well, we'll know more when we talk to them, I guess.'

Turning into the gates of the sprawling crushed gravel yards, Nick counted nine trucks parked in neat rows over beside the huge shed. All gleaming and shining in the sunlight, he noticed more flat top trailers than stock crates.

Pulling up to the front door of the transport yard's office, they got out and made their way over to the door of the small demountable building.

'Help you?' they heard from behind them.

He turned around and saw a neatly dressed man in light blue worn Levi jeans, and a freshly ironed navy-blue work shirt with a Turner's Transport logo embroidered over the top pocket. In his late 60s, he looked fitter than most of Nick's friends in the city who were his age.

'Morning mate, Detective Nick Vada, and Constable Joanna Gray. Mind if we ask a couple of questions?'

The elderly truck driver sipped his coffee in his left hand, and Nick noticed both hands were dark with grease.

'Nick Vada, pleasure to see you again mate, Greg Turner,' he said in Nick's direction, 'I'd shake your hands but I'm sure you don't want this grease on you,' he smiled, holding up a black stained hand.

Nick wondered when he would've met the elderly transport owner, and figured he probably knew his father. His question was soon answered, with the transport owner adding. 'I know your old man. Great bloke he is and can shear with the best of them. I actually gave you a ride in one of my trucks when you were a young fella.'

Nick had vague memories of a large red truck covered in chrome, and being fascinated by the size of the large bed behind the driver's cabin. With leather padded walls and tiny windows, it felt like a small house that he could play in.

'I think I remember that,' Nick said with a smile.

'Come into my office, I'll make you a cuppa.'

Nick and Joanna sat in the neat office, with photos of trucks adorning the walls, all with multiple trailers hitched on the back.

Greg pointed to one of the photos, a huge red truck covered in elaborate pinstriping, which was towing three long livestock trailers.

'That's the one I gave you a ride in.'

Cutting to the business at hand, Joanna asked, 'Greg, Russell Waterford told us one of your trucks was seen near his farm during the time we believe Rose Perry was murdered.'

'Murdered on his farm,' Greg said, finishing her sentence.

'We found the body on his property,' Nick said, knowing where the transport owner's train of thought was going.

'And he conveniently mentioned us when you questioned him?'

'Yes, he did,' Joanna said. 'We thought you may know something that could help us.'

'I would love to help, I truly would, but Russell Waterford has had it in for me for years.'

'And why is that?' Nick asked.

'Pretty simple, I started moving away from livestock and I've started carting solar panels.'

Nick wondered just what all of this solar panel business had to do with the murders, and if it had anything to do with his search for this killer.

Greg continued. 'Bailed me up in the pub about it last year. I was having dinner with my wife and kids. He was full to the brim as well, mind you; bloody embarrassing.'

'Why is it such a big problem for him?' Joanna asked.

'It actually has nothing to do with him,' Greg said, 'But he thinks I'm giving up on Milford and the traditional farming methods our generations of families have always used. Those methods were the reason I was almost broke.'

Nick wrote notes as the transport owner continued.

'And now I've got into carting solar. We've been busier than ever before, which I'm sure Russell sees. While he sits out on his farm waiting for the government to give him water, the old fool should just give up and get with the times.'

Joanna changed the subject. 'We heard a couple of your drivers have been in trouble up at Edithvale?'

'Ex-drivers. Tim McErny and Chris Jones. Got rid of them as soon as the Edithvale police came knocking on my door,' he continued with a sigh. 'I'm getting old guys. I have a family and I have no interest in any of that bullshit. I've only got a couple of years left, and I'll be putting this all on the market. Me or any of my boys didn't have anything to do with those poor girls' murders, and if there's anything I can do to help, I will.'

Nick felt like he was wasting his time and trusted the elderly transport owner. He felt like the interview had come to its conclusion.

'Thanks Greg,' he said, standing up, holding an outstretched hand and giving it a firm shake. 'I don't mind a bit of grease.'

'Anytime mate, have a good day.'

After heading back to the station, Nick got back in his car and began to unconsciously drive towards his childhood home on Evans Street. He cursed himself and wondered what he was missing. Had he put too much focus on Pete Waterford? Surely Pete didn't have anything to do with Taylor Dowd as well, absolutely nothing ties him to that scene. Nick himself had seen him at Warranilla that night, around the time of her murder. He knew the answer was somewhere in his head, with everything just not quite lining up yet.

Pulling into his childhood home, he found his Dad once again in the back garage, working on his black Holden ute.

'Making any progress?' he asked his Dad as he walked over the dead lawn.

'She's got a blocked jet in the carby, I reckon,' he said, holding an oil spray can up to the old, rusted carburettor.

'Need a hand?'

'Yeah, sounds good.'

Sipping on cold beer and watching the sun go down, he worked with his father on the V8 engine. He watched his father work and realised that his dad had probably forgotten more about engines than Nick would ever know.

He imagined what life would be like living in Milford had he never left. He'd probably be married to Jemma, maybe even have kids running around on his Dad's dead front lawn.

'You back on with Jemma?' his Dad asked, cutting through the silence, lighting a fresh cigarette.

Odd to talk about women with his Dad, he thought, unsure if he ever had before.

'It's nothing serious, Dad.'

'She's a keeper mate, I know you'll end up fucking off back to the city, so try not to break her heart.'

Nick bristled at the words. 'I won't Dad, I'm here to solve these cases now, nothing else.'

'Yeah, I get it mate, just offering some friendly advice,' he said, wiping grease off the back of his hand on his trousers.

Nick decided to ask his Dad the question that had been nagging him for the past few days. 'Dad, did Mum have any partners before she met you?'

He looked downwards towards the engine, taking another swig from his beer, and thought to himself. 'Hmmm, I'm not sure mate. We met pretty young. Your mother was from Edithvale originally. I met her at the local show.'

A smile now creeping onto his lips, he continued, 'An absolute stunner, my mates said,' his mind clearly back in those days. 'Why do you ask?'

Deciding to just get it out, he explained to his Dad about the case file he found all those years ago in Jack Thomson's garden shed, and his years in the police force running over the old file, hoping to one day find the identity of his mother's killer.

'The old cop shop burnt down in '94,' his Dad said, which was news to him. 'Jack told me he had saved a copy of the case file, maybe hoping he'd crack the case himself,' He chuckled. 'Not exactly the crack detective you are though, mate.'

He went slightly red at the compliment. 'Thanks Dad, I-'

'I know mate,' he said, 'But all this business of trying to solve your mother's murder is not healthy for anyone, I don't want you wasting your time trying to bring her back. I love her, and I miss her every day and that's all that really matters.'

'I know Dad, I just feel like the answer is right in front of me.'

'Well, try to focus on these women, mate. That's what you're here for.'

He excused himself to go to the toilet. He walked back over the dead lawn and through the back door of his childhood home.

After going to the bathroom, he began to make his way back out when an envelope on the kitchen table caught his eye. 'Edithvale Cancer Clinic - Urgent.' It was torn across the top already. Nick glanced out the back door towards the shed, and seeing his Dad bent over the bonnet of the ute, he unfolded the letter towards himself, and began to read.

To Mr TIM VADA,

I am writing to update you on the results of your latest test scan dated 1st October.

Unfortunately, Mr Vada, the growth in your lung has now grown to an inoperable size, doubling since your last visit in September. With no surgery being able to remove it, we ask that you return to Edithvale as soon as possible to discuss the next steps and how best we can make you comfortable.

Yours sincerely

Dr Campbell

His eyes widened as he read each sentence over twice to make sure he believed what he was seeing. His father was dying. Hours later, struggling with the news, he grabbed his phone and called his sister on his way back to his motel room.

'Jesus Nick,' Jess said to him quietly. 'Should we talk to him?'

'Well, the letter was dated two days ago, so you would think he would've already told us by now if he wanted to talk about it.'

'I don't know what to say,' she said.

'There's not a lot to say. We just need to be there for him as best we can, I guess.'

He thought to himself that despite the murders, he was grateful to be home while his father was so sick.

Turning into the motel parking lot, he saw Jemma sitting at the old plastic table and chairs with a bottle of wine in hand. A smile crept over his face.

Switching the car off and stepping out, he asked, 'Do you ever work?'

'Shop's open 8 – 2. We're in Milford Nick, It's country hours here.'

'Fair enough.'

Sitting on the old plastic chairs and sipping on wine out of plastic cups, he spoke to Jemma about his last few days, leaving out some of the grislier parts of the murders.

'I just don't understand why someone would want to kill either of those girls,' Jemma sighed, sipping from her plastic cup. 'Taylor was as nice as they come, and Rose, too.'

'Me either,' he said, still trying to keep his mind on the case and not look over at Jemma's toned arms.

'What do you know about the poker nights down at the football club?' he asked.

Jemma scoffed. 'All the footballers and old fellas in the town, playing cards and looking at young girls,' she said with a frown. 'Pete Waterford asked me once if I'd like to get involved. I nearly punched him.'

Nick couldn't imagine Jemma walking around topless, serving the men drinks.

'You should've,' he said, as he felt the wine starting to get to his head after all the beers he had drank at his Dad's house.

'You really don't like him, do you?' Jemma asked.

'It's not that I don't like the guy. I just don't trust him.'

'Is it because of what happened back when we were teenagers?' she asked.

Nick didn't like talking about what had happened back then.

'No,' he replied, almost too quickly. 'Never even thought of it.'

'C'mon Nick, I know you have. It was cruel, but we were kids. I wouldn't let it get to you. He's marrying your sister, so you're going to have to try to give him a shot.'

'Yes, yes, I know,' he said, draining the last of his cup, hoping to get off the subject of his awkward teenage years. 'Did you want to come in?'

'Hold up, cowboy,' she said with a wink. 'I have an early morning tomorrow. I better head off.'

He was slightly disappointed, but she walked over and kissed him full on the mouth, and he felt the stress of the day washing away.

'See you later,' she said, walking off into the darkness.

Chapter Seventeen

Nick was seventeen and felt like he was in the prime of his life. His Dad had helped him build his first car, a dark blue coupe with a loud engine, and he was sure that the girl in his year, Jemma Revell, liked him.

Sitting in the living room after Jess had gone to bed, he sat beside his old man, who had a can of beer in his hand, and the football on in the background. He sat and slowly mustered up the courage to ask the question he'd been thinking about all day.

'Dad?'

'Yeah?' his father said, though his eyes never came off the TV.

'There's a party out at the Rowntree's farm tonight, and me and Mick are planning on heading out.'

'Yeah?' His Dad said again, eyes fixed on the game.

'Any chance I could grab a six-pack for the party?' he asked and with no idea what his Dad would say next. 'Mick's Mum and Dad have bought him some.'

'Have they now?' he said, turning his eyes away from the TV.

He sat in silence with the only sound being the commentator's excitedly talking about the goal on the TV.

'Sure mate,' he replied with a small smile, as he drained his can. 'C'mon.'

He got up off the couch and made his way into the kitchen. Opening the old fridge and looking in, he said, 'Shit, you're taking out half my stash,' as he passed six cans over to Nick, who put them in his backpack.

'Don't drive if you're gonna drink that, mate. I've seen too many accidents from young blokes on the grog.'

Mick drove his ute, and Nick sat in the passenger seat, swigging from a bottle of rum that Mick had stolen from his parents and stashed in his glove box. Feeling it already starting to go to his head, he reached across and turned the rock music up loud.

'Take it easy Nick,' Mick said, with a worried look at his friend. He knew Nick hadn't drunk many times before and this party was his first big night out.

'I'm fine,' he replied, taking another swig of the bottle. 'Let's get this party started!' he yelled out the window into the vacant paddocks.

Mick pulled the handbrake as they turned into the entrance of the farm, with the rear wheels locking, the ute went sideways and slid neatly across the dirt road, then he unengaged it as he headed towards the table drain. Nick yelled out, 'Shit, nice moves Mick!'

'Years of practice,' he laughed, as he gunned the engine down the long dirt driveway into the dark night.

Seeing the glow of lights and fire in the distance, the boys soon came across the small gathering of people out in the paddock. Various cars and utes circled the fires, and some had headlights on to help illuminate the gathering.

The boys grabbed their alcohol from the back of the ute and began to make their way over to the fire drums and the direction of the loud music. Mick turned and spoke. 'Tonight's your chance, mate.'

Nick had been making his way out the front gate at school with Mick the previous day, when Jemma Revell turned and said to him at the school fence, 'Nick, are you heading out the Rowntree's tomorrow night?'

Nick, not even knowing there was a party on, was just about to say no, when Mick jumped in, 'The Rowntree's? Yeah, of course!' he replied, cutting his friend off.

Jemma looked over at Mick. 'Cool, I guess I'll see you there,' she said with a smile in his direction.

He took a long drink from his beer and looked over at Mick. 'Yeah, maybe.'

'Mate! C'mon! You've known her for a hundred years! It's pretty clear she likes you,' Mick said.

'We'll see what happens.'

The two boys made their way over to the closest fire drum where most of the local football team stood around. The Under 17s were reigning premiers and a couple of the players spoke to Nick because they knew their coach, Jack Thomson, was a family friend.

Standing separately over against the far fire drum were the girls. With faces full of makeup, short dresses, and high heels that definitely attracted the attention of the young boys across the way.

As Nick reached down for his third beer, he wondered to himself if he had ever drunk this much in his life. Probably not. The alcohol made him feel light on his feet and woozy.

As the night progressed and the two groups started to mingle together, and the music got louder and louder, he finally mustered up the courage to talk to Jemma. Walking over in her direction, he stumbled slightly as he got to the group.

'Nick, you ok?' she asked, as she looked at him with a worried look.

'Me?' Nick said, pointing to himself. 'I'm fine. You having a good night?'

'Yeah, it's fun. Want to get a drink?' she asked, as they moved away from the fire over to an old blue esky.

She reached down and pulled out a bright green coloured bottle and took a swig. 'Midori,' she said, holding the bottle out to him. He took a swig and felt the burning sensation on the back of his throat. 'Not bad,' he said, trying not to cough.

As the night went on, the two friends sat on a log away from the group and chatted about life. He felt more and more comfortable as the hours went on, and a lot more drunk. Looking into the horizon, he noticed headlights in the distance. 'Cops?' he asked Jemma.

'No,' Jemma replied. 'I think Pete Waterford and a couple of his schoolmates are in town. One of the footy boys invited him out.'

He hadn't seen Pete Waterford in a few years, but knew his parents were rich and owned the big farm, Warranilla, where his Dad worked from time to time, and that Peter would look down on Nick, being a private school kid. As the headlights drew closer, a large black expensive four-wheel drive pulled closer to the fires than any of the other cars. With music pumping from the speakers, the doors opened and a group of boys jumped out.

Watching the footballers greet the private school kids, he took another swig from Jemma's Midori. He always felt like an outsider in these situations, not being a football kid or in the popular group, and felt uncomfortable with the new group of arrivals who had turned up to the party.

Jemma and her friend went over to greet the new group and Nick held back, finishing his last beer. As he sat and waited for Jemma to return, he looked over at Pete Waterford. The centre of attention, he had a dark blue rugby jumper on with the white collar pulled up high, and a beer in his hand. Slowly making his way through the group of girls, he watched as he spoke with

Jemma. Definitely longer than with the other girls, Nick thought, as he felt his jealousy rising.

After watching Pete and Jemma drink and talk together for a couple more minutes, he noticed that Pete had laced his arm around Jemma's waist. He took a deep swig of Jemma's Midori and decided he'd had enough.

Standing up and realizing he was quite unbalanced on his feet; he made a beeline for the couple, who were now the centre of attention. As he stumbled over to them, he began to feel a wave of nausea hit him as the warm smoke went into his face and up his nose.

'Nick, you okay?' Jemma asked with a look of concern. 'Nick, this is P..'

'I know who he is,' he slurred in Pete's direction.

'Jesus, he's had a skinful,' Pete said.

Before Nick could think of a comeback, he looked down, and although he tried his best to hold it in, began to vomit all over the group's feet, with the entire contents of the night gushing onto grass and onto Jemma and Pete's shoes.

'Fuck me!' Pete yelled. 'Have a go at this bloke!' He jeered as all of his mates came over to have a laugh at Nick's expense.

Jemma looked at Nick, who had fresh sick all down his front. Her face full of worry.

'Might be time for spewy to leave,' Pete yelled to the party as the group cheered and hollered.

Mick half walked and half carried Nick back to his ute. He was now feeling more embarrassed than he had ever felt in his life.

'What did I do?' he asked Mick for the third time.

'You bloody power chucked all over Pete Waterford and Jem, mate,' Mick said. 'Might be best I get you home.'

He fell asleep immediately as he sat in the warm ute and hoped he would melt away and never be seen again.

Chapter Eighteen

Making his way back into the police station the following morning, Nick saw Joanna running to the front gate to meet him. Out of breath, she stood for a second and then said, 'You need to see this.'

Walking into the office and reading through the email on her computer, he finally felt things coming into place.

TESTING OF DNA ON EXHIBIT #4 LARGE HUNTING KNIFE

MR PETER WATERFORD 100% MATCH

He felt relief wash over him, knowing that his instincts must have been right.

'We've got him.'

He raced into the Sergeant's office with the printed email and the Sergeant's eyes slowly began to widen as he read the report.

'Head out to Warranilla. I'll get an arrest warrant from the Edithvale judge while you're on your way.'

Nick and Joanna got into the Milford police Landcruiser and began to speed towards the property, and soon headed through the large gates and down the gum tree-lined driveway. He stepped out of the Landcruiser as Joanna was still trying to park it. Heading down the pressed red brick path, he knocked on the front door of the homestead.

A wide-eyed Russell Waterford answered. 'Jesus Nick, what's the problem?' he said, after having watched the Landcruiser speed down his driveway.

'Where is Pete?' he asked.

'He's in the east shed repairing the header,' Russell replied, sensing Nick's urgency. 'What's this all about?'

'Show us the way,' he said.

Making their way in their cars past the side of the homestead, Joanna studiously followed the white Waterford Grain ute. 'Is the knife enough to convict him?' she asked the senior detective.

'It's enough to arrest him. Once the results from the fingerprints come back, that'll likely be the death knock.'

As Joanna followed the ute down the long dirt roads, and past the riverbank where Rose Perry's body was found, Nick wondered why no DNA had come up as a match for the first victim.

'Maybe your future brother-in-law was sleeping around?' Joanna asked, matching his thoughts.

Jess finding out that Pete was cheating on her could potentially be a decent motive to kill, he thought to himself. 'It's a possibility,' Nick said. 'I don't think the Waterfords would ever be happy until Pete married and settled down.'

Watching the Waterford ute slow, and turn left through yet another open gate, Joanna marvelled at the size of the property. 'It just seems to go on forever,' she said to Nick, looking out towards the horizon.

'Not something you would ever want to give up,' he replied.

Looking ahead to the end of the long dirt road, he saw the east shed rising in the distance, with a huge green John Deere header parked in the centre and the front tyre pulled off it. Pulling up and getting out of the car, Nick unclipped his handcuffs from his belt and walked towards the shed.

'Is that really necessary?' Russell Waterford said to Nick from behind him.

'Yes, I'm afraid it is.'

Looking beside the shed, he noticed two-pressure wash bays and a small tractor parked in one bay, being cleaned by a young farmhand. He made a mental note to request a search warrant for the shed once Pete Waterford was detained.

Walking past the back of the tractor and into the workshop, he noticed two doors ahead of him. The door on the left seems to be some kind of office, Nick thought to himself. As he got closer, he read the sign: 'The boss's office – keep out.'

'Jesus Nick, what's this all about?' Pete asked as he stepped out of the right-hand side door, wiping his greasy hands on an oily rag.

'Peter Waterford, I'm placing you under arrest for the murder of Taylor Dowd,' Nick said to the stunned farmer.

'What! Why? I didn't do it!'

As Nick approached him and made a move to grab his arm, Pete took a wide-ranging swing at him, which just grazed Nick above his left eye. Grabbing him by the elbow as he followed through, Nick spun him around and pushed him hard into the ground.

'Arghh, fuckin' hell, that hurt!' Pete yelled into the concrete.

'You'll be hearing from our lawyer for that,' Russell Waterford yelled at Nick.

'Self-defence,' he replied coolly, in the elder Waterford's direction.

With his knee on the farmer's back, he clipped the handcuffs onto his wrists. 'You do not have to say or do anything, but if you do, it may be used in evidence against you.'

'Fuck off! I didn't do it Nick!'

Picking Pete back up off the ground, Joanna led him to the back seat of the police Landcruiser.

'You're making a mistake,' Russell Waterford said to Nick in a serious tone he hadn't heard before.

'I'll be the judge of that,' Nick replied, walking past a wide-eyed Terry, the farmhand.

Making the long drive back down past the Warranilla homestead, his phone began to buzz constantly. 'Jess,' he mouthed to Joanna, who nodded silently.

'Nick! Mate! C'mon, I'm not a bloody murderer! I was with Jessie all night the night before last! How can I be in two places at once?'

Pete continued to protest his innocence for the entire drive back into town, getting angrier and angrier as they went. Turning into the carport of the police station, Jack Thomson came out to give them a hand. 'Put him in the lockup,' Nick said, pointing towards the back of the station.

Feeling his mobile still buzzing in his pocket, he finally answered.

'Nick, what the hell is going on?!' His sister yelled into the phone.

'Pete is under arrest Jess; I can't go into any further.'

'Bullshit!' she replied angrily, cutting him off. 'He didn't do anything Nick! I'm coming down now,' she said, hanging up the phone.

He was not looking forward to a confrontation with his sister, but she needed to understand where the evidence was taking them.

Hearing a vehicle pull up out front of the police station, he watched a clearly irritated Samantha Waterford, and the Waterford's lawyer, Harley Campbell, walking up to the front doors of the police station. Pushing through the door, and slamming it against the wall, Samantha looked at Nick with fire in her eyes, and asked, 'Nick, where is my son?'

'He is in a holding cell, Mrs. Waterford,' Nick replied calmly. 'And the only person he can speak to is his lawyer.'

Anger simmered in Samantha Waterford, who was clearly frustrated with Nick's answer. 'Harley, please let him know that his father and I believe him, and will do anything we can to get him out of this.'

'You have made your sister extremely upset, Nick,' Samantha Waterford said in his direction. 'She is absolutely beside herself.'

'I'm interested in finding out who is killing women in Milford, Samantha. I'm not too concerned for my sister currently,' he said, surprised at how harsh his words came out.

Leaving her in the front waiting room, he led the lawyer through the office and into the interview room. 'Wait here,' he said.

Walking towards the back of the station, he looked down at Pete sitting on the small cell bed. He looked like the adrenaline had finally left him, after his yelling in the back of the police car. 'I'm going to remove your cuffs, Pete, but no funny business.'

'Fair enough,' the crestfallen farmer replied.

Chapter Nineteen

Sitting down in front of Pete and his lawyer, Joanna turned on the recorder at the end of the desk.

'Constable Joanna Gray and Detective Sergeant Nick Vada commencing an interview of arrested suspect, Pete Waterford, November 6th 3:50pm,' she said into the recorder.

'Pete, can you please confirm your whereabouts two nights ago?' Nick said to the farmer.

'Yeah, I can,' he smiled. 'I was having dinner and a beer with you, if I remember correctly.'

Joanna raised her eyebrows in Nick's direction.

'After that, from 9pm until 7am the following morning.'

'I helped Dad load some grain samples into his ute, so he could head up to Edithvale in the morning, and then I shared half a bottle of wine with your sister and went to bed.'

'So, Jess, can verify your whereabouts?'

'Yep, I was with her the whole time.'

'Well then, how do you explain your DNA being found on the murder weapon of Taylor Dowd?' he asked, placing a photo of the blood-soaked hunting knife in the clear evidence bag on the table.

'Jesus,' Pete's eyes widened. 'Th-that's my knife,' he said, stammering, 'I use it when I go roo shooting.'

Peter was wide-eyed with shock, and Nick wondered whether he was genuinely shocked to see it, or if he was just a good actor.

'Can I ask then how we found your knife at the scene of Taylor Dowd's murder?'

'How the hell am I supposed to know? It could've been stolen out of the back of my ute. I'm in and out of town all the time. I wasn't there!'

'When we tested your DNA against this knife, your knife,' he said, holding the photo of the knife up in his direction 'We found your DNA match on it.'

'Well, of course you would,' Harley Campbell, the lawyer, interjected. 'My client has confirmed it is his knife. I'm sure through further testing you will find multiple DNA profiles on it,' he said matter-of-factly.

'We have done that,' Joanna said. 'The results should be back by the end of the week. Also, we are still waiting on fingerprint results from both crimes.'

'Well, as my client said in his last interview, which he attended of his own free will I might add,' the lawyer continued, 'I'm wondering if you have any other evidence tying my client to the crime scene other than this highly unlikely DNA match,' he said, pointing his pen at the photo.

'Pete, you spend much time down at the football club?' Nick asked, trying to change the subject.

'What's the football club got to do with this?' Pete asked. 'Me and my old man are major sponsors.'

'And you attend the local poker nights?' Nick continued.

'Yeah, from time to time, a few beers with the old man and a game of cards, even get a bit of a perv in,' he said with a smirk.

'I contend that you met the victim Taylor Dowd down at the clubs during these poker nights, and had an affair with her,' he said, watching Pete's mouth slowly open.

'Let me finish,' he held his hand up as Pete began to protest, 'When she found out you were marrying my sister, she threatened to tell Jess and expose the affair.'

Pete stared at Nick for a few seconds and broke into a hearty laugh.

'Is this honestly why I am here?' he said, between laughs. 'Mate, one thing you can't accuse me of is not loving your sister. Ask around, check my phone,' he said, throwing it on the table. 'I have nothing to hide.'

Joanna grabbed the mobile phone off the desk and walked out of the room with it.

'We will look into it further, Pete. In the meantime, you will remain under arrest.'

Nick took Pete back to his cell and then walked the old lawyer out to the front doors of the police station. Back in the office, he sat down beside Joanna at her desk, and watched her fingers flying up and down the phone screen. 'Gee, you know what you're doing with that,' he said to her with a smile. 'I'm useless on those things.'

'Gen-Y,' she said, with her eyes fixed on the small white screen. After five minutes of clicking messages and the odd email, she dropped the phone down on the desk and sighed, 'There's nothing, Nick.'

'Any texts or email. or anything suspicious?'

'No, I've read through all the texts on his phone and most of his emails, mostly to Jess and his mother. I think he really does love her,' she added, looking him in the eyes. 'Maybe he isn't our man?'

Nick got up and stretched his arms out one by one, and felt the small cut above his eye where Pete Waterford hit him, beginning to ache.

'That may be, but the DNA still matches on the knife at the scene,' he said, trying to rack his mind for something out of reach. 'And we still have the glove that has been sent off for testing as well.'

Looking over his shoulder and out the window, Joanna smiled. 'I think you better go deal with that.'

Turning around, and looking out to the carpark, he saw his little sister standing beside her car, with her phone up to her ear.

'Great, wish me luck,' he said.

Nick walked slowly out the front doors of the police station, with the sun shining in his eyes, not looking forward to the potential screaming match he was about to have with his sister. Leaning against the car with her arms crossed over her slender frame, she seethed at her big brother. 'Have you lost your mind? I already told you! Pete was with me the other night!'

'Yes, I heard you the first time, Jess, but we have found evidence which ties him to the crime.'

'What evidence? He wasn't there!' she yelled.

'Lower your voice Jess. We found his hunting knife, with his DNA on it at the crime scene.'

'Oh, fuck off Nick, you and I both know that knife could have come from anywhere! It could've been stolen out of the back of his ute!'

'Be that as it may, he's our number one suspect for now, Jess, and even with your alibi, we have enough to hold him.'

'Whatever,' she said, and got back into her car. 'I'm going to see Dad. Don't call me.'

'I'll talk to you later,' he said, knowing that although he had her fiancé in lock up, she wouldn't stay mad at him forever.

He walked slowly back through the doors to join Joanna sitting at the desk, still clicking through Pete Waterford's phone. 'Absolutely nothing,' she said, placing the phone back down on the desk in frustration. The young constable turned and looked at Nick. 'Shall we call it a day? Pub?'

'Sounds like a great idea,' he smiled, thinking that a beer would do him good.

Sitting down in the same booth in which he spoke with Jack Thomson a few nights earlier, he ran over the whole case again with Joanna, trying to pick holes in what they had come up with so far.

Sipping on a cold beer, he watched her play with her drink coaster, tearing the edges off it and dropping the pieces into the ashtray. 'Don't know why they even have these in here anymore,' she remarked, lifting up the chipped crystal tray. 'Haven't been able to smoke in here for years.'

'You know Milford is a bit behind the times,' he chuckled. 'Isn't that why you love the place so much?'

'Yeah,' she said, slowly sipping on her glass of wine. 'I guess it is.'

'Detective fuckin' Vada and Constable know-it-all,' came a loud voice, walking over from the main bar. 'Who let you in here?'

Daniel Matley had clearly had about eight too many drinks, and the night was still young. Sporting a fresh black eye, he slid into the booth next to Joanna. 'How are you going?' he said with a crooked smile in her direction.

'Fine, thanks Mr Matley,' Joanna replied. 'We were just trying to have a quie..'

'Pffffft.' Tiny flecks of spit hit Joanna in the face. 'Call me Dan, sweetheart.'

'Dan,' Nick said, swallowing the last dregs of his pot of beer. 'Might be time for you to leave, mate.'

'And what are you gonna fuckin' do about it?' The young footballer stood up. Standing up from his seat in the booth, Nick pulled himself up to his full height, a good foot taller than Daniel. 'I'm not going to do anything, Dan, but considering you're threatening a police officer, I'd choose your next steps very carefully.'

He watched the cogs tick over in the young footballer's brain and, not having to wait long; he broadcast it with a massive pull back of his fist. 'I don't fuckin' care,' he yelled as he swung wildly at the detective.

After being swung at for the second time in one day, Nick was more than ready this time. Quickly dodging the blow to his left-hand side, he was surprised to see what happened next.

He watched as Joanna swooped her leg out from the booth and hit Dan's knee with as much sideways force as she could muster. The young footballer screamed out in pain and hit the bar floor in a crumpled heap.

'Police business,' he said, holding his detective badge in the air as the patrons looked around curiously. Most slowly turned back to their glasses and continued with their conversations.

Pulling her cuffs out from the back of her belt, Joanna clipped them on behind the young footballer's back. 'I think you need to come down to the station with us.'

'Get off me, you fuckin' bitch!' Daniel yelled. 'This is police brutality!'

'You lot okay?' Marty asked as he walked around from the back of the bar.

'Fine thanks, Marty. He's had enough for the night,' Nick said, holding Daniel out in front of him.

Dragging the young footballer out through the front doors of the old pub, he opened the back door of Joanna's Landcruiser. 'Get in,' he said.

'Fuck you!' Daniel yelled in his face.

Nick pushed him hard, face first, onto the back seat, and he landed roughly with a dull thud. It had been a long day, and he was not in the mood.

'Charming,' he said to Joanna. 'Lucky we only had two drinks.'

Taking Daniel for the short drive back to the police station, Joanna pulled the Landcruiser into the front of the building. Walking to the back door of the car, Nick opened it up and roughly pulled him out.

'You're going to sleep it off in the cells tonight, mate,' Nick said to the young footballer.

'Whatever,' Daniel scoffed. 'You should be focusing your time on finding the killer in Milford.'

Pete stared in bewilderment as Nick pushed Daniel into the small holding cell.

'You two know each other from the football club? Looks like you'll be cell mates tonight,' Nick said, as he uncuffed him and pushed him into the cell. The young footballer was clearly confused by Pete being in the cell.

'Might be best we call it for tonight,' he said to Joanna.

'I agree.'

Dropping Nick off back at his motel, Joanna backed the large Landcruiser out of the driveway, and with a small wave, was gone.

Nick walked towards the door of his motel room and pulled the key from his pocket just as his phone began to ring. Pulling it out, he read the name on the screen: Jess.

Hoping his little sister didn't want to continue their argument from earlier, he answered. 'Jess, I'm in the middle of something. I can't talk.'

He could hear the sobs through the speaker on his phone. Through muffled cries, Jess spoke to her brother.

'Nick, it's Dad, he's dead.'

Chapter Twenty

The floor felt like it had fallen out from underneath his feet.

'What do you mean?' he said to his little sister, not knowing what she was saying. 'Where are you?'

'I'm at home. Jack's here with me,' she said through sobs. 'Please come as quick as you can.'

Knowing he had been drinking, he fired up his unmarked police car and flew down to Evans Street, well over the speed limit. Pulling up across the road from his old family home, he saw Jack's highway patrol car parked in the driveway along with his sister's hatchback and an Edithvale ambulance.

He stepped out of the car and made his way over the road in the moonlight. Taking a deep breath as he stepped over the gutter, and moved towards the home he grew up in, he saw the flashing lights of the ambulance casting deep blue and red shadows across the front windows of the house. How many more Vadas were going to die in this house, he wondered to himself.

Arriving at the front porch, he glanced over to the old timber seats and table where he had sat on with his Dad just a week earlier. He noticed Jack Thomson sitting quietly with his head in his hands. Jack slowly stood up and walked over towards Nick with tears streaming down his face. He gave Nick a big bear hug.

'I can't believe he's gone, mate,' Jack said, body trembling against Nick's.

'It'll be ok Jack,' he said, patting his Dad's best mate's back, unsure of what to say.

'In here Nick,' came the soft voice of his sister from the back of the house.

He walked slowly through the front door and down the hallway leading into the dining area. Two young paramedics sat at the dining table, quietly waiting, with the stretcher filling up most of the small room. Walking in through the kitchen, and towards the master bedroom, he found his sister waiting at the entrance of the room.

The argument earlier in the day felt like it was years ago. He wrapped his arms tightly around his sister. 'I'm sorry Jess, I truly am.'

He felt her sobbing against his chest. She pulled back and looked at her big brother, tears streaming down her face. 'He's in there,' she said, pointing through the bedroom door opening.

He took a deep breath, as his thoughts cast back to a couple of mornings after his mother's murder. Gingerly walking through the front door with his grandmother and little sister, he had made his way down toward the kitchen and the room at the end of the house where he knew his mother had been killed.

Unable to shake terrifying visions of blood-soaked walls and bedding, he heard his father call from inside the bedroom, 'I'm in here, guys.'

He had looked up at his grandmother with his eyebrows raised, and she gave him a small nod of encouragement. Grabbing his little sister's small hand, he walked towards the doorway of the room his mother had died in.

Stepping over the threshold and looking around for blood, he let out a sigh of relief. His Dad sat on the end of the bed with a sad smile. 'See? Nothing can hurt you in here guys, come here,' he said softly, with his wiry arms opening out wide, pulling them both into a tight hug.

Once again stepped over the threshold and into his mother and father's bedroom in what now felt like a lifetime later; still half expecting to see his smiling father still sitting on the end of the bed. His father lay on his side of the bed, with the covers pulled up over his thin and bony chest. Nick thought that his father looked like he was just having a sleep, if it wasn't for a small trail of blood running down the side of his mouth.

'I had to do some errands after we spoke,' Jess said to him, choosing not to mention their earlier argument. 'And then I thought I'd pop in with some Chinese and have dinner with him,' she said, unable to hold back more tears. 'I can't believe he's gone; I didn't think it would be so soon.'

Nick knelt down beside his father's body and held his cold rough hand, smiling to himself at the thought of their last night together. Drinking beer and working on his pride and joy.

'He would want us to be strong,' he said in his little sister's direction.

'I know,' she said. 'There's something else you should see.'

Walking into the bedroom door and closing them both inside the room, Jess pointed to the back of the door. His eyes widened. News clippings covered the door, from his first article in the local paper, signalling his intentions to leave Milford and join the force, all the way through to his last tumultuous year in the biggest case of his life so far to date in Sydney.

He marvelled at the collage of clippings covering his whole policing career, and wasn't surprised to feel hot, wet tears beginning to stream down his face.

'I know you had your differences, but he was so proud of you.'

'I know,' he said quietly, unable to control his emotions, feeling the tears stream freely from his eyes.

Turning back to his father's body and not caring that his little sister was in the room, he spoke to his father.

'I know you can hear me, Dad. I'm not going to stop, I'm going to find out who killed Mum whether it's the last thing I do.'

He turned to Jess and spoke to her. 'Let's go. I think Jack needs looking after more than I do.'

Walking back out the bedroom for the last time, he watched as the two quiet paramedics wheeled the stretcher through the kitchen and in towards the bedroom.

Creaking open the screen door, Nick could see the Sergeant, now sitting quietly by Jack's side.

'Came as soon as I could,' he said, quietly in Nick's direction. 'Absolutely anything you need, you let me know.'

His initial distrust in the old **Sergeant** beginning to dissipate, Nick looked at him and said, 'Thanks, I appreciate you being here.'

'No worries at all mate, if you need some time off I can speak with the **Chief**.'

'No. I think sticking to the case will help keep my mind busy.'

'Understood,' replied the **Sergeant** quietly. 'C'mon Jack, Let's get you home mate,' he said to the old highway patrolman, standing up and wrapping his arm over his shoulder.

'Joanna may need your help down at the station; an extra prisoner,' he said to the **Sergeant** as he walked away.

'Already been down there. She's got it under control. She's a good girl, that one.'

Nick looked back at his little sister, not quite knowing what to do next. The events of the day had finally hit him, and he rubbed his temples slowly, and then his eyes, trying to clear all the troubling thoughts in his head, and the craving he had for alcohol.

'Whoa, are you ok?' Jess said, noticing him sway.

'Yeah, I'm fine.'

'You need sleep,' she said in her best motherly tone. 'Let me drive you back to the motel. I would invite you out to Warranilla, but I'm not quite sure you're welcome there at the moment.'

'Motel will be fine thanks smart arse.'

They hopped into the small hatchback, and began to make the short drive back to the motel. Jess was the first to break the silence.

'The paramedics said his heart finally gave out. With the cancer so badly spread, it must have caused a heart attack.'

Nick said nothing, still unable to believe his father was gone. He was running out of family members, and the thought made him feel more alone in the world than ever.

Breaking the still silence in the night, his phone began to ring. Pulling it out of his pocket, he answered, 'Hello?'

'Hi Nick, it's Joanna, I'm so sorry for your loss, the Sarge just called.'

'Thanks, Jo.'

'Look, I know it's not the best time, but I just finished processing our friend in for the night, and got an email with our fingerprint check on the knife.'

'And?' he said, expectantly.

'There are fingerprints on the knife. But they are from an unidentified perpetrator. It's not a match.'

Chapter Twenty-One

He ran his hands through his hair and rubbed his temples in frustration. Shit, he thought to himself. 'Damn it, thanks, Jo.'

'Everything ok?' Jess asked, sensing his frustration.

'Yeah fine, just some updates on the case.'

'Well, hopefully you will let Pete go. Now I've given you an alibi,' Jess said.

'Yes, it's all being taken into consideration. Let's talk about it tomorrow, yeah?'

Turning into the carpark of the motel, he noticed a Waterford grain ute parked further along the lot towards the end of the building. 'Looks like the motel has doubled its capacity.'

'Looks that way,' Jess said, looking towards the ute. 'I think that's Russell's car. He must have had business in town.'

As he pulled off his seatbelt and began to open the car door, Jess continued. 'I'll start organising the funeral, not many deaths in Milford these days. I'm guessing it will probably be Friday,' she said, obviously forgetting all about the two recently murdered women.

He didn't feel like it was time yet to be worrying about funerals, but knew all people dealt with grief differently. His sister was the organiser, always had been. 'Thanks Jess, I'll talk to you tomorrow.'

Stepping out into the cool night air and making his way into his motel room, he headed straight for the bathroom and ran a hot shower. Taking off his clothes and stepping into the old bathroom shower, he let the hot water slowly run down his face, grimacing slightly as it ran over the graze where Pete Waterford had hit him earlier on in the day. If Pete didn't murder those girls, then who did? Was it Daniel Matley all along? Or was there someone else quietly lurking in the shadows? The day had once again produced more questions than answers, and he could feel another headache coming on.

He switched the shower off and made his way over to his bed. Cracking two more Panadol tablets, he walked over to the ancient fridge and opened it up, staring at the bottle of rum he had bought the day previous. Deciding against a drink for once, he lay down and tried to close his eyes. With his mind full of thoughts and memories of his Dad, he fell into a restless sleep.

Waking up in the morning, he was pleased not to have a hangover. That's better, he thought, stretching his arms up over his head. Not needing to pop any more tablets, and with a clear head, he showered quickly and got dressed. Pulling his phone off the charger, he checked his messages, reading the top one from Jemma: 'Heard about your Dad, Nick. I'm so sorry, I'll be at the shop if you need me.'

He left his car keys on the bench in the old motel room and made his way out the door. Looking to his left, down towards the end row of the motel, he noticed the Waterford grain ute was nowhere to be found. Back down to one occupant, he thought to himself, wondering just how the small motel could possibly make any profit.

He made his way on foot down the short stretch of highway that ran into the end of the main street. Stopping to wait for two cars to pass, he recognised the bright white of Samantha Waterford's Mercedes SUV as the second car of the two. Looking through the windows, he noticed Samantha Waterford driving, and in the passenger seat, deep in conversation was another one of the Chinese businessmen he had seen around. What was that all about?

Turning onto the main street in the cool morning air, he saw
only two 'open' signs: Joe's Bakery and Revells. Walking
towards the shopfront, he almost collided with Russell
Waterford, as he walked out of the bakery with a coffee in his
hand.

'Shit, I didn't see you there,' he said to Russell. Eye to eye
with the old businessman, he realised that Russell could've
passed as Pete's brother and not his father; he still looked just as
sharp and fit as his son.

'Morning Nick,' Russell said with a cold smile on his face.
'Thank you for releasing Pete. I'm sure this was all just one big
misunderstanding. No hard feelings, mate?' He held an
outstretched hand to Nick.

He couldn't believe what he was hearing. Trying to maintain
his composure, he shook the rough landowners' hand. 'None at
all, Russell,' he said, matching his smile. 'I'm just trying to do
my job,' he added.

'When you actually find the real killer, I'm sure Samantha
and I would love to see you back out at Warranilla,' Russell said.
'In the meantime, however, stay away from my family.'

'I'm not finished yet, Russell. We have just found some more
evidence which is pointing us in the right direction,' he said with
confidence, hoping the older man wouldn't call his bluff.

Russell's eyebrows raised slightly at that. 'Pete didn't do it and unless you feel like losing your sister forever, I'd suggest you leave him out of it.'

He said nothing, hoping his sister's loyalties would remain with him.

'And also, I'm sorry for the loss of your father,' he added, shaking his head slightly. 'He was twice the man you are.'

Russell walked past Nick and out of sight toward his ute. Nick rubbed his temples and closed his eyes for a short moment. Knowing he now had one of the biggest landowners in the region - and someone who was meant to be a future family member - as an enemy, was causing him to start questioning his line of investigation.

'What was that all about?' Jemma asked, as she stood in the doorway of the shop, looking beautiful as ever.

'Just friendly conversation,' he said, annoyed he didn't think to ask the landowner about the Chinese businessman.

'Nick, I'm so sorry about your Dad,' Jemma said with a deep sadness in her eyes.

'Thanks Jem.'

He walked into the warm shop, escaping the cool morning air and embraced Jemma in a tight hug. 'It just doesn't feel real.'

'If you need absolutely anything, I'm here for you,' she said.

'I know you are. Thanks.'

He left the shopfront and continued his walk down the end of the main street. Continuing past his childhood school, Milford High, and down past the local park, he made his way to the police station. Walking through the front door, he made a beeline for the Sergeant's office.

The Sergeant spoke first, 'First of all, you shouldn't be here mate, and second, I know,' he said, with his hands up in a mock sign of surrender.

Joanna was leaning against the filing cabinet in the corner, in dark jeans and a small tight t-shirt. Nick looked over in her direction with a questioning stare. 'It's my day off,' she said, shrugging. 'Nothing better to do.'

'Samantha Waterford posted bail this morning for him,' The Sergeant said. 'We only had the DNA on the knife and he didn't lie to us mate, it's his knife. Samantha showed us a photo of him holding it.' He pushed an image over the desk in his direction. 'But with the fingerprint evidence coming up as not a match, we didn't have anything else to go.'

'I've sent the fingerprints back to Sydney hoping to get a match through the whole Australian database,' Joanna said.

'For the meantime, then, we have nothing,' Nick said with frustration in his voice.

'Looks that way,' the Sergeant replied.

Nick sighed and looked over towards Joanna. 'Let's have a chat with our young footballer friend again, shall we?'

'Can't wait,' she said with a smile on her face.

Walking down through the office and towards the back of the lockup, he smiled as he looked through the bars at Daniel Matley, who was kneeling beside the toilet, green in the face.

'Have a bit too much to drink last night, did you mate?' Nick said in Daniel's direction.

'You don't say,' he replied sheepishly, his fresh black eye now a deep shade of purple.

'I'm going to ask you a few more questions, and then I'm going to let you out all right?' he said, leaning against the cool bars of the lockup.

'Sounds good to me.'

'When was the last poker night down at the football club?' he asked, flipping his notepad out of his pocket to a fresh page.

'Three weeks ago, on a Thursday night,' Daniel replied.

'Anything suspicious happen that night or anything different from usual?'

'Nothing that I can remember, besides coming second for the night and taking everyone's money,' he smiled. 'There was one thing, though,' he said, wiping his chin.

'Yes?' Joanna asked expectantly.

'I was cleaning up at the end of the night, and I was going through the back kitchen where the girls get changed, and out beside the bins I saw Rose and Waterford having a pretty heated argument. He had a wad of cash out and was waving it in her face.'

'And did you say anything to them?' Nick asked.

'Yeah, I told them to cut it out, and that we are all friends here. I think Rose was relieved to see me, actually,' he added. 'She looked a bit frightened. I asked her about it afterwards, but she blew me off.'

He underlined the argument with Rose in his notepad and made a point to speak with Pete again.

'Thank you, Dan,' he said, unlocking the lock and throwing his phone over to him. 'You are free to go.'

Getting up gingerly and grinning at Joanna, Daniel winked at her on his way out and said, 'I'll see you later constable.'

'He gives me the creeps,' Joanna said, shivering in the cold lockup hallway.

'I think he has the hots for you,' he said, trying to contain a laugh.

'Yeah, no thanks.'

'Let's head down to the football club again and have a look around,' he said to Joanna, hoping maybe to find some more evidence.

Heading back down towards the football club in Joanna's Landcruiser, he looked over at the young constable, wondering to himself if she had anyone in her life. 'You seeing anyone?'

Unable to see her eyes through her dark sunglasses, Joanna said, 'Who's asking? My boss or a friend?'

'I'm not your boss. We're partners.'

A smile spread wide across her face, and she continued, 'I appreciate that. My goal is actually to become a detective like you one day.'

'Well, you've certainly got the right stuff to make a great detective.'

Blushing, she replied, 'Thank you, and for your first question, no I'm not seeing anyone.'

'Well, Mick Perkins is single. His wife passed away a couple of years ago. I could arrange dinner?'

'I prefer to do my own work, thank you,' Joanna said, with a cryptic smile, ending their conversation.

Turning into the entrance of the football club and over the small bridge, Nick could make out in his side mirror the back end of a white ute tray, speeding away from them in the opposite direction towards the other end of town.

'Jeez, he's in a hurry,' Joanna said, seeing the same thing through her rear-view.

'I'm sure if he keeps driving like that, Jack will catch up with him,' he said, hoping his Dad's old friend was doing okay today.

Pulling up at the back of the clubrooms, he walked inside the building, using a set of keys he had borrowed from Jack's drawer back at the station.

Inside and looking at the wall of old photographs, he saw many faces he recognised, including a photo of him and his old friend Mick Perkins who had played one season in juniors; Jack Thompson in his glory days; and many of his old school friends celebrating wins throughout the years.

'Doing some reminiscing?' Joanna said, cutting through the silence.

'Yeah, I guess I am,' he said with a smile on his face. 'Better times.'

Continuing down the wall, he came across Jack Thomson, holding a premiership cup high in the air with a massive grin on his face. His muscles bulged out the side of his football jumper, and the whole group was looking at him with big smiles. His Dad had said to him Jack was one of the best country footballers Milford had ever seen.

Looking closer at the photo, he recognised his father, standing against the fence with his mother by his side, both smiling from ear to ear. It was another photo of her he hadn't seen before. Seeing them both so happy made him smile. Trying to see if he recognised anyone else in the photo, he noticed close to his mother's side were Samantha and Russell Waterford.

'Let's check out the other side of the oval,' Nick said to Joanna. 'Maybe the killer left something else behind?'

Walking across the wide football oval which sat only 200 metres from the river, he looked out at the dark green waterway in the distance. The town's water tower rose up through the gumtrees, dark rusted steel beams holding up the shining tank.

'What's on the other side of the river?' Joanna asked, pointing at the dense clump of gum trees lining the opposite riverbank as they made their way down into the tree line.

'Farmland,' he replied, 'I think that's the Turner's place. It was once part of Warranilla.'

Walking through the gum trees and looking through the long grass, Joanna replied, 'Far out. I didn't think that place could have been any bigger.'

As the words came out of her mouth, Nick heard a loud bang and fizzing noise. The trunk of the gum tree above their head, and to the right, exploded in a shower of bark and leaves.

'Get down!' he yelled, pushing Joanna to the ground and dropping down as fast as he could.

'Did we just get shot at?!' she yelled at him.

'Yes, we did,' he answered, straining his eyes in the direction of the gunfire. Seeing the unmistakable reflection of a rifle scope shimmering in the distance, he could just make out a figure running back through the tree line.

'When I tell you, get up and run,' he said quietly to the scared young constable.

Feeling the adrenaline running through his veins that he was more accustomed to in the city, his instincts remained on high alert. Not seeing the figure through the tree line anymore, he grabbed Joanna by the arm and yelled at her to run. 'Now!'

Jumping over the oval fence and making their way back to the security of the football clubrooms, Joanna said with a heaving chest, 'Jesus, I can't believe we just got shot at.'

'It means the killer is still out there, and somehow, we must be getting close.'

Chapter Twenty-Two

Nick watched as the Sergeant used a pocketknife to pry the bullet out from the old gum tree. Digging deep, he finally managed to get it out.

'Looks like it was a 223,' he said, holding the bullet up in the sunshine. 'Most popular gun in these parts.'

'What are they used for?' Joanna asked.

'Roo shooting,' he answered, knowing his Dad had one in his gun locker in the back of his shed. He then remembered that it was now his gun.

'Well, that doesn't narrow it down at all,' Joanna said, disappointed. 'Could be anyone's gun.'

'We can send the bullet away for testing and if the gun has been used in a crime, we will be able to get the owner of the gun,' he replied. 'Although it's not likely.'

'I'll head out to the Turner's farm and have a look around, see if Neil saw anything,' the Sergeant said to Nick, dropping the bullet into a clear evidence bag and removing his latex gloves. 'I'll send this off as well. Talk to you two later.'

Nick's phone began to ring in his pocket. Pulling it out, he noticed another unknown number. 'Detective Vada?'

'Nick! Mick Perkins here, mate. Got your number from Jemma!'

'G'day Mick,' he replied, thinking about his conversation earlier in the day with Joanna.

'Sorry to hear about your old man, mate. Fancy a counter lunch at the pub? Meet in halfa?'

'Yeah, sounds good,' he said. He thought that after the morning he'd had, it might be a good time to clear his mind for a few hours with an old friend.

'Great! See you then.'

He hung up the phone and turned to Joanna. 'I have a couple of jobs to do this afternoon. Can you drop me off back down the street?'

'Yeah, of course,' she said. 'I think I need a lie down after all of the action today.'

Getting dropped off near the Coachman's Inn, he made his way across the road and through the old corner door and into the main bar. The same four old bar flies from the night before sat at the end of the bar with ice cold pots of beer in hand.

'Sorry to hear about Tim,' one said, raising his glass in Nick's direction.

Marty, the barman, nodded, and the four men raised their glasses in a quiet toast. 'To Tim.'

'Thanks boys,' he nodded in their direction. 'How did you know my old man?'

The oldest of the four men had a long grey beard and sat in the corner of the bar. Propped up next to the window, his arm hung out in the street with a cigarette in hand. He technically wasn't breaking any laws, Nick thought to himself.

'I was a wool classer for many years up at the Turner's farm, and I worked with your old man in those sheds day and night,' he said, taking a sip of his glass of beer, and then a deep inhale of his cigarette.

'Your Dad never did the big numbers, but he was the most consistent shearer I'd ever seen, a hundred a day, every day I ever worked with him. Young blokes would come and go, shearing a hundred and fifty, and laughing at him, but they'd be on the floor the next day after the first fifty. Your Dad would just pluck away, cool as a cucumber, doing the same hundred as the day before,' the old man said, with a twinkle in his eye.

He had never heard much about his father's shearing exploits, with his Dad being a man of few words. Listening to the old men talk about their time in the sheds with his Dad he smiled, and really started to appreciate him even more, knowing that whenever he could be at home, there would be a hot dinner on the table ready for him and his sister, all while working such a hard and physical job. He hoped that he could be half the man his Dad was.

Hearing the bar door open behind him, he saw his old friend, Mick Perkins, walk in. Arms outstretched and pulling him into a big bear hug, Mick said, 'I'm bloody sorry mate.'

'Thanks Mick, I'm glad I was here.'

'Yeah, the timing is bloody lucky, I guess actually, although you're not here under the best circumstances.'

Walking back through the main bar and into the bistro, the two old friends took a seat. Noticing two younger women sitting at the table across from them, he saw the taller, tanned blonde looking in their direction.

'Backpackers, I'd say,' Mick said, looking over towards their table. 'You always had your way with the ladies mate,' he said, chuckling.

'I think she's after you, mate,' Nick said, watching the blonde's eyes looking in Mick's direction.

'I'm too bloody busy at work to worry about that sort of stuff. Look at me,' he laughed. 'Do I look ready for a date?'

'How about my partner, Jo?' he asked.

Mick sipped his cold beer and smiled a devilish grin in his direction. 'We may have been in touch already.'

He laughed at his mate and knew that losing his wife at a young age had affected him more than anyone would ever know.

'Mate, you know I've been through exactly what you have before,' Mick said, referring to his late wife. 'Anything you need at all, please let me know.'

'Thanks Mick, I appreciate it.'

'Now, what do you want to eat? I don't even need to look at the menu. Get me a chicken parmi.'

Walking over to the bar, he spoke to Marty, 'Two chicken parmis please, mate, and two beers, thanks,' he said, tapping his card on the EFTPOS machine.

Walking back with two cold beers and placing them on the table, Mick was the first to speak. 'So, will I be getting my apprentice back on the job?' he asked, talking about Matley.

'It's up to him, mate. He's lousy on the drink but I don't think he's a killer.'

'I didn't think he would've had it in him either,' Mick said. 'But what would I know? I'm just a welder.'

'You're more than that,' he said. 'Look at how well you've done.'

'Nearly gave it all away and headed to the mines with Dean when I lost her,' Mick said.

He thought back to his old friend's close friendship with Jemma's ex-partner. 'How's he going up there?' he asked.

'Making an absolute killing like everyone, but you wouldn't see me out there in that heat welding pipe all day. I'm making the same money here doing my thing.'

'And how long is this Chinese money going to last? I had dinner out at Warranilla the other night, and Russell Waterford was telling me that the new government is going to come in and give the farmers all their water back.'

'Yeah, he would say that,' Mick scoffed. 'He knows all the movers and shakers in government, so what would I know?'

Nick said nothing.

'Although, a little birdie tells me Warranilla may be up for sale,' Mick said.

'What?' he said, surprised at the revelation.

'Yeah, apparently Samantha Waterford has floated the idea to Sheng Holdings. They're the same company that I build the solar panel bases for. Keep it between you and me, but their CEO is flying in from China next week to meet with her, I hear.'

He couldn't believe what he was hearing. 'Is Russell Waterford involved in the deal?'

'Haven't heard his name mentioned,' Mick said, draining his beer. 'Another?' he asked, pointing at the empty glass.

'Yeah righto,' he answered. 'What about Pete Waterford?'

'Nah, no one else,' Mick said. 'Only Samantha has been involved, that I know of.'

Nick filled his old friend in about the multiple sightings he had of the Waterford matriarch, chatting with the businessmen and wondered what, or if, it had anything to do with the murders in town.

'Yeah, well there you go,' Mick said, mouth now half full of chicken parmigiana.

'What sort of money would it be worth?'

Swallowing the large chunk of chicken, Mick replied, 'Shit I don't know, I'd say north of ten million, you've got the river running through it and it's the widest and flattest section of land in the state, mate. If they sold it I'd have work building those solar panel bases for the rest of my lifetime.'

Taking a bite of his own meal, Nick sat in silence, wondering who was to benefit from the sale and just what the Waterford men would possibly do without the farm to work on. 'Well, call me old-fashioned,' he said. 'But I hope they don't sell. It's the last large local homestead owned by a Milford family.'

'Yeah, yeah, I get history, but the future is coming Nick, and it's all solar.'

Chapter Twenty-Three

Nick left his old friend at the pub perched up next to the four barflies and wondered what his next step should be. He had both the murdered girls on his mind, and the pieces of the puzzle were laid out before him. Knowing that the answer was within reach, he knew that there was just one missing piece that would pull everything together.

As the sun began to set and he started to walk back towards his motel, he found himself out the front of Jem's shop. Tossing up whether to continue on his walk back to the motel or go in and see Jemma, he decided on the latter.

Making his way down the small laneway beside the shop, he slowly walked up the rickety timber stairs leading up to the small apartment. As he raised his fist up to knock on the door, the door opened, revealing a smiling Jemma standing on the inside holding a bin bag. 'Take this out, would you?'

After making his way down the stairs and dropping the bag in the rubbish bin, he made his way back inside and sat down on Jemma's deep blue suede couch. Cricket on in the background, he asked who was winning.

'Beats me,' she said, handing him a glass of red wine. 'How was your afternoon?'

He sighed. 'Not bad, had lunch with Mick Perkins.'

'How is Mick?'

'Same old Mick,' he laughed, telling Jemma about the smiling backpackers and pushing his old friend to try to meet someone new, like Joanna.

'Sounds like I had some competition.' Jem smiled in Nick's direction. 'Should I be worried?'

'Not at all,' he said, feeling the wine go to his head, joining the beers from lunch. 'You know you've always been the girl for me.'

Jemma took a long sip from her glass of wine. 'And you've always been the man for me.'

After a dinner of lamb and salad cooked by Jem, he sat back down on the couch, rubbing his stomach. 'If I keep eating like that, I'll need to buy bigger pants.'

'Well, you know where to buy them,' Jemma replied.

Sitting quietly, sipping their wines together and watching the cricket, Jemma turned and lay her long, tanned legs in his lap.

'Have you ever considered moving back here?' she asked, with hope in her eyes.

'Not really,' he said and watched the hope extinguish, 'Although after a week here already I'm certainly coming to realise I miss the place more than I thought.'

'Well, there are things here that miss you as well.'

Falling back into a quiet contemplation, they sat together on the couch while he stroked her legs on his lap. He hadn't felt at peace like this for a long time; he thought to himself, as he sipped his wine. No other responsibilities in his life, except for the case at hand.

The next morning, he got up from Jemma's bed and quietly got dressed, hoping not to wake her. Walking through the kitchen of the small apartment, he noticed a black suit jacket, pants, and white dress shirt draped over a chair, with a post it note: 'For you. See you later today.' Nick smiled to himself and grabbed the suit.

Slipping out the rear doors of the apartment, he made his way down the stairs and into the cool morning air. Starting to make the walk back to his motel room, he heard his phone ringing in his pocket. He looked down at the screen and saw the name of his Chief.

'Morning Chief,' he answered, unsure why his mentor from Sydney would be calling at this time of the morning.

'Nick, morning mate, I just heard the news about your old man. How are you doing?'

'I'm all right, thank you,' he answered, appreciative of the Chief's call.

'I'm sorry for your loss, and I'm worried about you, mate. All of this is a little too close to home for my liking. Did you want to head back to the city and have some time off?'

'No chance, Chief,' he said with defiance. 'I have to see this through.'

'Fair enough,' the Chief sighed. 'You're the best I've got, mate, so if anyone's going to do it, it'll be you.'

'Thanks.' he replied, hanging up the phone.

After showering at the motel and changing into his new black suit, he saw his sister's small hatchback pull into the motel carpark. Getting out of the car, she walked into his room. Wearing a black dress with her hair pulled into a high ponytail, she looked her brother up and down.

'Ready?' she asked.

'As I'll ever be.'

Hopping into the car, they made their way over to the small chapel that backed onto the local football oval. The only other time Nick could remember being here was for his mother's and grandmother's funerals.

The small white chapel sat nestled in the shade of three large paperbark trees, with one leaning precariously close to the old church roof. The building looked like it was overdue for a renovation, he thought to himself, with the high-pitched gable roof covered in old mossy tiles, cracked and weathered all over. Pulling into the carpark, he was surprised at how many cars were already there, sighting two Waterford grain utes parked in the shade.

'Pete coming?' Nick asked, already knowing the answer.

'Of course, Nick,' Jess replied, not looking for a fight today. 'He is my fiancé, after all.'

'After all of this?'

'Yes, after all of this, as I said the other day, he is innocent, and I plan to be his wife after all of this blows over Nick. Dad loved him and I'm sure one day you could too.'

He thought that hell would freeze over before he trusted Pete Waterford, but didn't want to get into an argument on the day of his father's funeral.

'We'll see about that,' he said quietly.

Stepping out of the car, he saw Jemma walking through the parking lot, looking beautiful in a neat black dress. Quietly smiling at Nick, she spoke to his sister first. 'Hey Jess, I'm so sorry for your loss,' she said, giving her a hug.

She turned and gave Nick a kiss on the cheek and interlocked her arm with his. Eyebrows raised at the couple, Jess said, 'Shall we?' and pointed to the entrance of the church.

The three walked silently through the doors of the church. As they made their way down the aisle, he looked through the crowd at the people he knew.

The **Sergeant** and Joanna sat in full uniform in the third row, with Mick Perkins and two more of his old friends, James Reynolds and Alex Baggett, each giving him a sad smile and nod. Looking further towards the back row of the church, he saw the Waterford family, all impeccably dressed, with Russell Waterford wearing a black Akubra matching his dark suit jacket. Samantha Waterford wore a long black dress with a small sapphire pin clipped on her chest above her heart, and Pete Waterford finished off the row in a neat, dark navy suit.

Jemma sat in the front row by Nick's side, with Jack and Nell Thomson on Jess's side. They sat and listened through the service, with Jack making everyone chuckle during Tim's eulogy.

At the end of the service, Jack got up once again to speak to the small gathering. 'The football club will be open later on this afternoon for the night. If anyone would like to come along and celebrate Tim's life, I know he would love to see us all there enjoying a beer.'

****

Later that night down at the football club, Nick sat in a chair with Jemma by his side. Pouring his sixth beer for the day, he felt the alcohol hitting him instantly, the cold beer making his head feel better. It had been one of the worst weeks of his life; losing his Dad, being shot at, and feeling like the case was slipping out of his grasp. He grabbed the second full beer bottle on their table and began to take long drinks of it as well, feeling in a self-destructive mood.

'Don't you think you should slow down a bit?' Jemma said to him quietly, with her eyes full of concern.

Draining the bottom of the bottle, he looked over in her direction, 'What's the point?'

He wondered why he was still even in Milford anymore. Maybe he should have just listened to the Chief and headed back to Sydney. Someone else should take up the case, he thought.

Walking back up to the bar for yet another beer, he tripped slightly and bumped into the back of Jack's shoulder.

'Jesus mate, it's not a competition,' Jack said, looking at Nick swaying on his feet. 'Maybe try to slow down a little,' he continued, looking worried at Nick's behaviour.

'You're not my Dad,' he replied angrily.

'No, I'm not,' he said sternly, 'But I made a promise to your Dad when you got back here that I would look after you.'

'I don't need looking after,' he said. 'I can handle myself.'

'Fair enough,' Jack said with a sad look on his face. 'Let's talk later, mate.' He disregarded Nick and turned back to the group of men he was talking to. Nick grabbed another beer off the bar and walked over towards the wall of photos in the clubrooms. Standing close to the photos and chatting with a group of people with drinks in hand, were Russell and Samantha Waterford.

'Nice of you to come,' he said, with sarcasm in his tone evident.

Russell Waterford turned towards him, and noticing how drunk the detective looked, raised an eyebrow. 'You okay there Nick?'

'Me?' he said, pointing to himself. 'I'm fine.'

Pointing at the photo on the wall between the couple, he asked them, 'Did you know my mother?

Sam grimaced slightly. 'Yes, we did, Nick. She was a good friend at one stage of my life.'

'And what happened between you two?'

'Just the usual things that happen with young people. I was away a lot with university, and we grew apart,' she said as Russell watched their conversation intently.

Pete excused himself from another group and walked up to Nick from behind. 'What's happening over here?'

Noticing what was happening, Jemma walked over and grabbed Nick by the arm. 'Nothing at all Pete, just friendly conversation,' Jemma said with a smile.

'Yeah, just trying to find out who is killing women in the town,' Nick said in Pete's direction.

'Excuse me? You'd want to watch your tone mate, you're not on the job at the moment,' Pete said, warning him.

'I'm always on the job,' he said, spilling his beer down the front of himself.

Nick decided he had enough. Who was Pete Waterford to come to his father's funeral? And to speak to him like this?

'Well, maybe you need to do better because there's a killer still walking around amongst.'

Pete didn't get a chance to finish the sentence. Nick pulled his arm back, and before Russell Waterford could intervene, delivered a crushing left hook to Pete's chin.

One of Pete's bottom teeth came out and Nick saw a trail of blood fly out of his mouth as he fell backwards towards the wall in slow motion.

'NICK!' screamed Jemma.

'Get him out of here!' yelled Russell Waterford, rushing to his son's aid.

'Jesus Nick! yelled Jess, running over to the commotion. 'What have you done?'

Nick's drunken haze snapped away in that one short moment. Realising the repercussions of what he had just done, he looked blankly at the scene before him. Not knowing what to do next, he turned and decided to leave. Nick walked towards the door but blocking the exit was the **Sergeant** still in full uniform, with his arms folded and a disappointed look on his face.

'Mate, I think you better come with me.'

Chapter Twenty-Four

Nick woke up groggily, still in his black suit, and wondering where he was. Looking at the bright fluorescent lights above him and the steel bars of the Milford police lockup cell, the day before's events started to come back to him.

Shit, he thought to himself, what the hell was he doing, getting drunk at his own father's wake? He couldn't believe he could be so stupid. He had embarrassed himself, and what was left of his family.

'Morning,' said a quiet voice from behind the bars. Joanna stood in her uniform, watching him sleep.

'Morning,' he replied, full of embarrassment. He was unsure what he could even say in this situation.

She opened the door of the lockup cell with a quiet turn of the lock. 'Sarge wants to see you in his office.'

He slowly got up, feeling the tightness in his back from sleeping on the hard mattress. 'Thanks,' he said as he walked past the young constable.

Walking down to the office, he saw the Sergeant seated at his desk, with Jack Thomson leaning against the filing cabinet.

'Morning detective,' he said sternly, pointing at the chair in front of his desk. 'Take a seat.'

He took a seat and looked at Jack and then across to the old Sergeant.

'Mate, I know you've had a rough go at it losing your Dad and all, but what you did last night was absolutely unacceptable.'

'Sarge, I know, let me.'

The Sergeant raised his hand. 'Let me finish. I've spoken with your Chief Inspector, and he has decided you need some time off, mate. He expects you back in Sydney by Monday. We have a new homicide detective coming down to take over.'

Nick couldn't believe what he was hearing. 'Sarge, you can't take me off it. Yeah, I was drunk. And I made a mistake, but I can feel it. We are this close,' he said, holding his fingertips close together.

'Not my call mate,' replied Sarge. 'Leave your gun and badge here, and I'll post them up to Sydney for you.'

He stood up and made his way quietly out of the office. Joanna looked expectantly towards him from behind her computer screen and he shook his head. 'I'm off the case.'

'I thought as much,' she said sadly.

Not having anything else to say, he walked out the door of the police station and headed back to his motel room. The heat of the morning sun was cooking him in his black suit, and he could feel like alcohol seeping out of his pores. What the hell was he going to do now? His chance of solving the case was now non-existent. Back at the motel room, he put his flat mobile phone on the charger and lay down on his bed, with his head still pounding from the alcohol and bad decisions of the previous night. Unsure of what his next move should be, he heard his text messages start to chime.

Picking up his phone, he saw that he had multiple missed calls and messages. He read the first and most important message from the Chief.

'Disappointed in you, detective, please make your way back to Sydney. Your car has tracking, so I'll be watching you. No detours.'

He lay on the bed and closed his eyes. The motel bed felt like a palace compared to the jail cell, and he soon fell back to sleep. Snapping out of his nap, he stared at the ceiling, feeling disappointed in himself and his actions, but knew that he could still solve the case. He just needed more time. But how was he supposed to follow any more leads with no car?

A lightbulb went off in his head. Grabbing his phone and changing into casual clothes, he once again set off on foot out the motel door, closing and locking it behind him.

He made his way back down the main street and over to Evans Street, to his childhood home. Opening the screen door and pushing the front door open, he chuckled to himself. No one lives here, and it's still open.

Making his way down the hallway and through the kitchen, he decided not to look through the opening of the master bedroom door, unable to comprehend his father was now gone too. He continued out through the old back screen door, over the dead lawn and to his father's shed. Pulling up the tilt panel with a loud screech, he looked down on the old ute, shining as it sat idle in the shed. With its bonnet closed and keys in it.

He stared silently at the ute and knew his Dad would understand that he needed to borrow it. Threading himself in the driver's side door, he turned the V8 engine over.

'C'mon, old girl,' he said, as he willed the ute into life.

He was beginning to wonder if the old ute may not start when he finally heard a small cough from under the bonnet, and the V8 engine roared to life. Rumbling quietly in the back shed, he could feel the tin on the roof reverberating around him as he clicked the ute into gear.

Slowly creeping the ute out of the shed and closing the door behind him, he marvelled at the shine of the paint on the vehicle, now rumbling quietly in the sunshine. It truly was a beautiful machine, he thought to himself, getting back in the driver's seat.

Turning out of the driveway and looking at the sun as it sat high in the sky, he thought of the one place he hadn't been yet been during his visit to town. Rumbling slowly down Evans Street as the old ute continued to warm up, he slowly accelerated and made his way toward the south end of town.

Heading off the southern highway and past the local pool, which was now desolate and empty, he felt the ute's tyres bounce down onto the dusty dirt road. As the sun was getting lower and lower on the horizon, he pushed the accelerator down hard into the carpet and felt the old engine spool up. Feeling like he had been shot out of a cannon, he smiled as he felt the adrenaline running through his veins as he flew down the dusty dirt road on his way to the Milford cemetery. His dad was out there in the dirt somewhere, and he smiled thinking about how happy he would have been to see the old ute out and about.

Slowing down gradually, he pulled up to a stop close to the front entrance, and was the only car in sight. Turning the engine off and getting out, he made his way through the gates. The cemetery was surrounded by barbed wire farm fencing to keep away any stray kangaroos.

Making the same walk he had completed many times in his life, he came upon the grave of his mother. The grave stood silently, dwarfed by the marble angel standing behind it. He had always wondered who had organised the marble angel, with his father and sister having no idea who had paid for the beautiful memorial to his mother. He knelt down at his mother's headstone and saw a fresh bouquet of flowers sitting neatly beside it. Who would have left this here? He thought to himself, as he picked the flowers up and smelt their scent. Looking for a card, he found none, and gently placed them back down against his mother's headstone.

Looking out into desolate paddocks, he spoke to his mother, cutting through the silence. 'I messed up **Mum**, bad. And I don't know what to do. I know if you were here, you would have helped me.'

As he sat and thought about all the stupid decisions he had made over the past few days, he began to feel a renewed vigour in trying to get to the bottom of what was happening in his hometown. 'Someone is killing women, **Mum**,' he said. 'And it's my job, no matter what, to get to the bottom of it.' He sat in silence for a beat and then continued, 'And I haven't stopped searching, **Mum**. I will find your killer.'

Heading back to the motel again with a thought kernelling inside his mind, he pulled the old ute into the carpark beside his unmarked police vehicle. Walking into the room, his ears perked when he heard the word 'Milford' on the news report, with stock footage of his hometown flickering on the old screen.

'Police are currently investigating the murder of two women in Milford,' the news reporter said. 'With shocking similarities to the Murray River Killer, Jim Hooper.' Bullshit, he thought, but who was he to get in the way of a good story?

'Channel Four reports that members of Sydney's elite homicide squad have been tasked with investigating and are making headway on the case. More to come in the late-night news.'

He turned the TV off and stared up at the wood-panelled ceiling. With the last few weeks running through his mind like a television show, he flashed through the scenes in his head and tried to grasp at something, anything, that could help him with the case. Like a lightbulb in his head, it hit him. His conversation with Terry the farmhand about washing Pete Waterford's ute the night before Rose's murder. How could he be so stupid? He had completely forgotten about the conversation with the young farmhand and couldn't believe he hadn't followed it up.

Now formulating a plan, he made his way back to his dad's ute, he needed to be organised by nightfall.

Chapter Twenty-Five

Nick stopped at Joanna's small unit behind the main street and knocked lightly on the door.

'Coming,' said a voice from behind the door.

Opening the door and squinting in the bright sunlight, Joanna looked out at Nick. 'Thought you may have already left.'

'Nah, thought I'd stick around for a bit.'

'Oh yeah? And what do you plan on doing?'

'Finishing this,' he said.

Joanna's eyebrows raised at this, and he knew that she wanted to know more. He knew what he was planning to do and didn't want to incriminate his young partner so decided to keep his plan to himself.

'There are still the fingerprint results to come back. Who knows, we might get a break,' she said, with not a lot of confidence.

'Hopefully. But in the meantime, I'm going to get us evidence they can't refuse. Don't tell Sarge or Jack I've visited. I will see you tomorrow,' he said cryptically, making his way back to the ute.

As he got into the ute, he heard his phone ringing. He hoped it wasn't his Chief or the Sergeant. Seeing Jemma on the screen, he smiled and answered, 'Hello?'

'Hey.'

'Hey Jem.'

'Hi. Jack told me you've been stood down and are heading back to Sydney?' she said, with sadness in her voice. 'I can't believe you punched Pete Waterford, Nick. What the hell were you thinking?'

'I guess I wasn't,' he said. 'But I'm not leaving just yet.'

'Please make sure you come and see me before you go.'

'I will.'

Making one last pickup before his midnight trip, he headed back up into the driveway of his old family home and walked back into his Dad's garage. Opening the cobweb-strewn side door with a loud screech, and making his way towards the back of the shed, he stared at his Dad's old gun safe.

He quickly found the keys sitting on top of the safe. Great security Dad, he thought. He opened the door expecting to see multiple guns, but only found a single rifle left. Sitting in the centre of the safe was his Dad's favourite weapon, the well-oiled and pristine Winchester, 22/250. He picked the vintage rifle out of the gun safe, marvelling at its beautiful condition. Once owned by his grandfather, it had been passed down to his Dad, and now down to him, he guessed. Slinging it over his shoulder, he took the box of bullets from the top shelf. If someone was going to take potshots at him again, this time he'd be ready.

Walking back out with the old rifle, he carefully laid it behind the black leather bench seat and got back in the ute, with the trusty V8 engine firing up again easily after it had remained warm. 'I'll look after her, Dad,' he said, touching the worn steering wheel.

He had waited for the sun to set on the horizon, and once it was fully dark, he quickly stopped in at the small service station he'd first stopped at when he'd got to town. After filling the ute up from near empty, he walked into the service station and found old Earl Mason sitting at the register reading the local paper.

'Hi young fella, sorry to hear about your old man,' Earl said, not looking up from the paper.

'Thanks Earl,' he replied, with childhood memories flooding back, of coming to the service station for lollies with his little sister.

'Too young he was, although he got more years in than your mother.'

Not sure what to say, he asked Earl, 'Did you know my Mum?'

'I did,' he said, flipping the newspaper closed and looking him in the eye.

'I was mates with Russell Waterford back in the day, and he and your mother used to date.'

Nick had thought there was something between them ever since he saw the bakery photo. 'How long for?' he asked Earl.

'Oh god mate, I dunno', he and Samantha were on and off all the time and so was she with your dad. It was a different time. That'll be $90,' he said, pointing down at the EFTPOS machine.

He tapped his credit card to pay for the petrol.

'Technology,' huffed the old station attendant.

'Thanks Earl.'

'Look after that ute young fella, there aint' many of them left.'

He fired the old ute up and turned onto the main highway, with his thoughts lost in the past. Mind racing, he wasn't quite sure what to make of Russell Waterford and the news that he and his mother had dated.

As he drove through the dark night, with his headlights on high beam, his mind continued to mull over everything that had happened in the past week. The murder of Rose, Taylor coming to him asking for help, her murder and his father's death, and then finally, being shot at from the riverbank. Something must tie it all together, he thought to himself, as he tried to search for the missing piece of the puzzle.

With Warranilla beginning to come up in the distance, he switched his headlights to low beam and began to slow down. He drove past the main homestead gates and continued on his way to a second entrance he knew, where he hoped no one else would see him. Coming up over the rise, he found the gate easily and turned off the main highway, onto the old dirt tractor track that led to the gate.

Quickly opening the gate and driving his ute through, he continued along the rough dirt road until he hit the main graded gravel track that connected the main sections of the farm together. Driving slower now, and hoping his headlights and dust wouldn't alert anyone, he slowed down as he approached the wash bays beside the east shed. Seeing the shine of the huge John Deere tractor still parked in the shed, he slowly parked under a giant gum tree and turned off the ute.

Waiting to hear the noise of anyone approaching, he sat in the ute with the windows wound down slightly, hoping to hear the hum of any vehicles on their way down to the shed. After a few quiet minutes, he slowly opened the door and grabbed his father's rifle, loading a bullet into the chamber and putting five more in his top pocket.

It was so quiet as he walked, he could hear the blood rushing in his ears in the bright moonlit night, feeling like the snap of a twig could alert people at any moment. He could feel sweat beginning to develop on his back, which made him cold in the frigid night, and a shiver ran through his body. As he crept slowly towards the wash bay, he stopped and waited, listening in the silence. Feeling like someone was watching him, he couldn't shake the feeling that he had already been found out.

Entering the wash bays and trying to not make noise, he noticed that one of the Waterford grain utes was parked in the wash bay already. He quickly pulled out a pair of rubber gloves from his back pocket and making his way to the door, he tried to open it.

'Shit,' he said to himself as he lifted the handle and felt that it was locked. He had wanted to move the ute back and search inside the drain of the wash bay.

Hoping the keys may be in the back of the ute, he slowly unclipped the tailgate and searched inside the tray. He pulled out old lengths of rope, a bag of fertiliser, and some muddy gumboots. Looking next to the wheel well, he noticed a long leather knife sheath with the handle of a knife protruding from it, almost identical to the one found at the Taylor Dowd crime scene. Interesting, he thought as he reached into his pocket for a handkerchief then carefully grabbed the handle and pulled the knife out towards himself. As he unclipped the leather press stud and pulled the large blood-stained knife out from its sheath, his eyes widened at what he saw.

Still attached to the end of the knife was the small bloodied, ripped section of Rose Perry's white sundress.

Chapter Twenty-Six

I knew it, he thought to himself triumphantly; finally knowing he had enough proof to nail Pete Waterford for both of the murders. Realizing that the news would devastate his sister, he felt no satisfaction with what he was about to do.

Walking back to his ute, with his gun slung over his shoulder and sheathed knife in hand, his mobile phone rang loudly and he scrambled to silence it. 'Shit, shit, shit,' he said to himself, trying to answer the phone before anyone was alerted.

He answered the private number with his voice barely more than a whisper. 'Hello?'

'Nick! It's Joanna, I've been trying to get onto you!'

'What is it?' he said quietly, trying to keep his voice low in case anyone was around.

'It's Russell Waterford, Nick!' Joanna said, with her voice full of panic. 'His prints took a while to come back as a match because they were so old! From his time in the army! He's the killer!'

As he was about to reply, he heard the now familiar crack of gunshot that he'd heard when he was down by the riverbank with Joanna. Soon, he heard a bullet fizz menacingly just past his head and smash into a nearby gum tree. As he began to run towards the old ute, he hoped against all hope that he could get the hell off the farm before he was caught.

Hearing the whip crack of the gunshot go off again as he ran, he began to feel a searing hot pain in the back of his calf muscle, and the pain was now making its way up the back of his leg. He felt like his whole right leg was on fire. Looking down, he realised to his shock that he had been hit, and a large patch of blood was beginning to show through his pant leg.

I just need to make it to the ute, he thought to himself. Adrenaline coursed through his veins now he knew Russell Waterford was the killer, and from what he could gather, the gunman shooting in his direction. As he heard the third crack, he thought that his time may be up. With the bullet entering his right shoulder, he fell forward and smashed his head against the back-left corner of his father's ute.

This is the end, he thought to himself, dazed and confused as he saw the headlights of a ute slowly ambling over to him. Soon after, he fell into an unconscious haze.

Feeling water being splashed across his face, he opened his eyes up and realised he was sitting in the east machinery shed, with Russell Waterford standing in front of him. His eyes struggled to acclimatise to the brightly lit space, and soon he began to feel a burning pain in the right side of his body. He looked down and saw that he had lost quite a lot of blood, with a pool of it dripping slowly down from the ripped shirt sleeve on his right arm. Trying to move his arm, he realised he was tied to an old office chair, with his hands behind his back.

'You just wouldn't stop, would you?' Russell Waterford said, looking down at him with a long hunting knife in his left hand.

'I knew you were getting close, but I thought my shot at you near the club rooms might have scared you off.'

Nick's mind was a haze of pain, and he struggled to comprehend that the elderly landowner was the killer of the young women. With his head aching and his body on fire, he felt he may fall into unconsciousness at any minute. Still feeling slightly confused, he asked Russell, 'Why?'

'None of this should ever have happened,' he said as he leered over Nick with the knife pointed at him.

'The minute she told me she was pregnant, I should've just gone and told Sam and got it over and done with.'

'That *who* was pregnant?' he said slowly, already knowing the answer. He could feel all the loose threads in his mind slowly starting to finally connect.

'Rose,' Russell said, sitting down on the old leather chair opposite him.

'You and Rose Perry were together?' he asked, still struggling to believe what he was hearing.

'It wasn't just the poker nights and the money,' he said sadly. 'She said I really knew how to make her smile.'

'So, what happened then?'

'We met at the poker nights,' Russell continued. 'She was a bloody knockout, Nick. She looked like one of those catwalk models. She would come over and sit down on my lap. Good evening Mr. Waterford, she'd say with that million-dollar smile. I felt like I was the president or something.'

'Go on,' he said.

Realising the ropes behind his back were slightly loose, he began to try to quietly wriggle them from side to side and begin to loosen them. With his right arm still on fire, he could feel the blood running freely from his wound and onto the old ropes behind him.

'Then we began to meet up. She'd come and stay the night at my motel, Room 11,' he said, looking at Nick. 'Best sex of my life mate.'

He now realised why the Waterford grain ute was constantly parked at the motel for the business meetings the clerk had told him about.

'So why did you kill her?' he asked, feeling the knot wrapped around his right hand beginning to slightly loosen.

'Because she got fucking pregnant!' Russell yelled, standing up again. He quickly stopped playing with the knots.

'And she comes to me in the middle of the night and tells me she wants to keep it! I said no, of course. And then she tried a different tack. She said if I wasn't going to financially support her and the baby that she was going to drive straight to Warranilla and tell Sam about the whole thing!'

Nick grimaced. 'Russell, you had plenty of other options other than murder. Do you really think your life is worth more than an innocent woman's?'

'There was no way Sam was going to find out!' Russell yelled in his direction. 'She's trying to sell the whole fuckin' farm from underneath me! I know she's talking to those Chinamen,' he said.

'So why didn't you just sell the whole farm and move on with your life?' he asked, beginning to try to loosen the knots again.

'Because I'm not a fuckin' quitter like you and the rest of this town,' he snarled. 'You left your family and moved on from Milford. I could never leave this farm. It's in my blood.'

He decided to change the subject. 'And what about Taylor Dowd?'

He scoffed. 'Little bitch tried the same thing as Rose did on me. Obviously, Rose told her about the pregnancy and she came to me a few nights later trying to blackmail me for the same thing! I thought I'd got her down by the pub, but you intervened. I got her down by the grandstands though,' he said, waving the large knife in the air. 'She screamed like a baby roo when I put the knife in her.'

Nick felt the knots around his hands go loose. Trying to think of what to do next, he continued the conversation. 'All of this death, and for what?' he asked. 'This town has seen enough murder already. First my mother, and now these women,' he said, hoping to glean information from him.

Russell frowned slightly. 'That one I don't know about,' he said. 'It's a damn shame she.'

Nick was just about to jump from his chair to try to tackle the knife away, when he heard the crack of a gunshot come from behind him. He watched as the bullet entered Russell's shoulder, and he fell to his knees as blood began to pool across his shirt. 'What the hell?' he said in complete shock.

'POLICE!' shouted Joanna and the Sergeant, as they both ran in with their guns drawn at Russell Waterford.

'Get on the ground!' the Sergeant yelled at Russell as he pushed him on the ground and cuffed him.

'You ok mate?' The Sarge asked as he walked over and untied Nick from the chair.

'Russell Waterford, you're under arrest for the murders of Rose Perry and Taylor Dowd,' Joanna said with satisfaction on her face.

As he heard the words come from Joanna's mouth, he felt like the floor was beginning to fall away from him, and he felt himself going in and out of consciousness. With the amount of blood loss he had suffered; he felt uneasy on his feet. He decided he needed to sit down, and as he walked back over to the chair he'd been tied to, he collapsed, falling hard on his right shoulder, with the pain of the fall knocking him out.

'Shit! Nick!' Joanna yelled. 'Call the ambulance!'

His next memories were a blur, with visions coming to him in spurts. Flashing blue and red lights, a dark moonlit night, paramedics fussing over him as he tried to protest that he was okay, and then nothing but black.

****

As he slowly felt himself coming back into consciousness, his eyes ached at the bright fluorescent lights above him. Opening his eyes fully, he looked around and realised he was in a hospital bed, with Joanna and his sister sitting in the chairs beside him, deep in conversation.

He looked down and saw his right arm in a sling, and felt the lightness of the heavy painkillers running through his bloodstream. 'Where am I? he asked.

'Nick, thank God you're okay,' Jess said, as she ran to the bedside. 'You're in the Edithvale Hospital.'

'I'm fine,' he said with a weak smile at his sister.

'You've been shot twice,' Joanna said as she walked over to his bedside.

'Two times too many,' he said with a laugh, slightly coughing and wincing in pain.

'Just rest Nick,' Joanna said. 'We can talk about what happened when you're better.'

'How'd you know I was on the farm?'

'I tracked your phone,' Joanna said, holding her phone up.

'We got the fingerprint results back late yesterday afternoon. Russell Waterford had his prints on file when he was sent to Vietnam. Being such old records, they are usually the last ones the database takes into consideration.'

'And we've got the knife off the machinery shed floor. It is being tested for Russell's DNA and fingerprints along with the rigging glove we found at Taylor Dowd's murder scene.'

'He made a full confession to me,' he said.

'Yes, we know. He has offered a written confession to the Sarge as well. I can't believe it. I really thought Pete Waterford had something to do with this.'

'Me too,' he said. 'Looks like I have some apologising to do,' he said with a sigh as he looked over in his sister's direction.

*****

After three days in the Edithvale hospital, much to his sister's annoyance, he checked himself out, knowing he had unfinished business in his hometown.

Pulling up to the front of Warranilla in his Dad's old ute, the late afternoon sun had begun to set in the distance with the gum trees casting dark shadows across the burnt ground. Turning the keys off in the ignition, he slowly opened the door and got out with the pain in his leg, causing him to wince.

Standing on the front porch in her dressing gown Samantha Waterford spoke in his direction. 'Tim?' she asked, with a confused look on her face.

Slowly limping up the red brick footpath, his right arm in a neat sling, he appeared battered and bruised after his time in the east sheds. 'Hi Samantha,' he said sadly, 'Did you think it was my Dad?'

Looking like she didn't know where she was, she looked at him in confusion. 'I'm sorry Nick, I haven't seen that old ute in a long time.'

'Let me help you inside Samantha, we'll make a cup of tea,' he said, interlocking his arm under hers.

Walking through into the rear living room, he saw his sister and future brother-in-law sitting together at the small dining table.

Sitting down at the table with the two Waterfords and his sister, he filled them in on what had occurred out in the east sheds and Russell Waterford's confession. Afterwards, the four of them sat in silence in the large room, sipping their cups of tea. No further words needed to be spoken.

Nick was the first to break the long silence, looking towards Pete.

'Pete,' he said, trying to find the words. 'I don't know what to say. I followed the clues, and I was totally wrong, and for that, I'm deeply sorry.'

'It's okay mate. You were doing your job. You even had me second guessing myself for a minute there.'

After falling back into silence for a second time, Pete then continued, 'I thought there may have been something going on with Dad and Rose. I saw him arguing with her out the back of the football clubrooms when I was taking a leak behind the grandstands.'

He thought back to his chat with Daniel Matley in the lockup. 'I'm an idiot,' he said to himself.

'Why?' Pete asked.

'I spoke with Daniel Matley after his night in the lockup, and he told me that he saw Rose arguing with 'Waterford' and my mind went straight to you,' he said, pointing in Pete's direction. 'Turns out he meant Russell Waterford. Would've saved me a whole lot of heartache if I had clarified that,' he said, feeling stupid.

Samantha Waterford hadn't said anything since he told her the whole story, and he could see tears streaming down her face.

'I just don't know why he would do it,' she said, referring to the affair.

He remembered the solar project and the Chinese businessmen. 'He told me you were planning on selling the farm?'

'Yes, we were,' Sam said, looking in Pete's direction.

'It would've been a life-changing amount of money. Russell is getting old,' she said, and then continued, 'And his days of working on the farm were numbered.'

'Something to discuss over the next few weeks,' Pete said to his mother. 'There are still memories to be made here,' he said, smiling at Jess.

Nick looked at his sister and then Pete, content that his sister was in safe hands.

'Thank you, truly,' Samantha said to Nick. 'If you didn't get to the bottom of this, no one would have.'

He smiled sadly at Samantha.

'Just doing my job.'

Chapter Twenty-Seven

Nick got back into the old Holden ute and fired up the engine. Turning back onto the gravel driveway, he wound the windows down and listened to the sound of the V8 engine rumbling through the warm country air.

He made his way back into town, with the magnitude of the past week's events finally beginning to hit him, as waves of tiredness crashed over him. He pulled into Evans Street and then turned into the driveway of his childhood home.

Making his way slowly over the dead front lawn, up the steps, and through the open front door, he settled down on his father's couch and turned the TV on, his eyes heavy. Closing his eyes, the painkillers he had taken earlier did their job and he soon fell into a deep sleep.

Slowly waking and hearing the sound of the TV in the background, he rubbed his eyes and realised it was the morning. The sunlight came through the old windows and shone on his face. Getting up and walking into the kitchen, he filled the kettle up from the kitchen tap and put it on the boil. Standing in the small kitchen, he wondered what his next step should be.

After draining a large mug of black coffee, and finding a pack of Panadol on the top shelf of the pantry, he turned the TV off in the lounge room and walked out the front door, locking it behind him.

Standing on the front porch, he looked up at the sky; the heat of the day already starting to make the air around him feel like warm soup. Walking down over the dead front lawn, he stopped and turned, looking at the state of the tired gardens. Wrestling with an old, cracked garden hose and sprinkler, he left it spraying over the front lawn. 'That should help,' he said to himself, not ever having his own lawn when he moved to the city.

Firing up the ute, he made his way back to his motel room. After showering and packing his bags into the boot of his police car, he walked over to reception and dropped the key off through the slot.

Cruising down the street, he noticed two of the old shearers from the pub sitting out in front of Joe's bakery. Both giving him a big wave, he greeted them with a wave and a smile on his face. Parking at the police station, he took a deep breath and turned the ute off.

'Never thought I'd see it out of the shed again,' Jack Thomson said, leaning against his highway patrol car beside him. 'I don't think I'll check the registration today either,' he said, winking at his old friend.

'Jack, I wanted to apologise for my actions the other day,' he said, wanting to clear the air.

'Too much beer, mate, happens to the best of us. No harm done. How's the wing?' he said, pointing at Nick's arm in a sling.

'Getting there.'

Pointing towards the police station, he replied, 'Better get in there mate, I think there's a badge in there with your name on it.'

He walked past his old friend and made his way back into the police station.

Joanna greeted him at the entrance. 'Welcome back. How are you feeling?'

'Thanks. Good to be back. I'll be alright.'

Walking back through the door and into the office space, he made his way over to the Sergeant's office.

'Nick,' the Sergeant said, 'Take a seat,' he said, pointing at the chair in front of his desk.

The Sergeant started. 'Well, obviously you broke multiple laws last week in your little excursion out to Warranilla.'

'I know, I know, but I just knew deep down that something was going on out there,' he replied.

'Let me finish, mate. Like I said, multiple laws were broken, but I have updated the Chief Inspector on your exploits out there, and left out a few key details. The Chief has agreed with me that your actions were fully justified, and he has decided to give you your badge back.' He pulled Nick's gun and badge out from his top drawer and slid them over the desk.

'Thanks, Sarge, I really appreciate it.'

'The Chief has spoken with me further and said he thinks it's best if you take a few weeks off before you come back to work. I'm sure there will still be a wedding to attend in the next week or two.'

His mind had been so tied up with the murder investigation that he couldn't believe he had forgotten about his sister's impending wedding. 'Yes, I guess there will be, although I'm not sure what I will do in Milford while I wait.'

'Go take that ute out with your lovely lady and enjoy yourself mate. God, after all of this action, I might just retire.'

His mind circled back to the last thread of unfinished business he had in Milford. 'Sarge, considering I'm going to be here a few more weeks,' he braced himself. 'I'd like to look into my mother's murder.'

The Sergeant sipped his mug of coffee thoughtfully and looked him hard in the eyes before placing it back down on the bench. 'It's a quiet town, Nick. I'm not stopping you. After the fire in the station, we don't have many paper records left, but I'm happy for you to try. You can take Joanna along if you need assistance.'

He felt relief wash over him, hoping that he could finally, maybe, get some closure on his mother's death.

'Oh, and one more thing. The chief decided after Joanna's great work and help in detaining Russell Waterford, it might be time for a promotion. I thought you might like to give her the good news.'

He smiled and thought about the young constable. Her hard work was paramount in helping solve the crime. 'Thanks, Sarge, it'd be a pleasure.'

Nick walked back out of the office and over to Joanna's desk, unable to keep the smile off his face. Watching the young constable type away at the screen, he sat down beside her. 'I have news.'

'Oh yeah? You got your job back?'

'Yes, I'm a detective again,' Nick added. 'And I'm talking to Milford's newest Senior Constable.'

Joanna's smile widened. 'Oh, really? Thank you so much.'

'You deserve it,' he said, sliding her new name badge across the desk.

'I thought I may be Milford's newest detective. After you were stood down, it was either me or Jack.'

Nick smiled. 'Well, I'm back on board and I have a new case I'd like to solve.'

'Oh yeah, what's that?' she asked.

'Yeah,' he continued. 'My mother's murder.'

Chapter Twenty-Eight

Joanna looked at Nick with a sad smile on her face.

'I heard about your mother's murder,' she said. 'The Sarge filled me in when we heard that you were in town.'

'Unsolved and not much to go on,' he said with a sigh. 'But I'd like to ask around a few different people and see what I can find out.'

'I'll be happy to help,' Joanna replied.

Sitting back in the dining room of his childhood home, he filled Joanna in on the details of the case, handing the old manilla case file over to her and watching her silently flick through the pages, with concentration etched on her face.

'The wedding ring,' she said, reading Detective Jason Peters notes in the back of the folder. 'It has to be somewhere?'

'Whoever has that ring killed my mother,' he said, looking back at her.

'Is this all that remains of the investigation?' she said, holding the flimsy folder up. 'It's not much.'

'It's all we have,' he said sadly. 'There has to be something, anything, in there that can help.'

He sipped his coffee thoughtfully. Surely someone knows something in this town. His mother couldn't have been murdered over a wedding ring. He then remembered his conversation with the old fuel station attendant he'd had before making his way out to Warranilla. 'I think we need to speak with Earl Mason,' Nick said, filling Joanna in on the conversation.

'It sounds like a start,' Joanna said. 'Let's go.'

'Wait a minute,' he said, as he walked out the rear door of the house. 'Something I need to do.'

He walked around the rear of his Dad's old garage and found a second hose and sprinkler, unfurling it out around from behind the shed and plugging it into a tap.

'Doing a bit of gardening?' Joanna asked from behind him, standing at the rear door.

'Mum always had this garden looking immaculate,' he said, as he turned the tap on the back garden hose.

'And it may be a small thing, but I'm going to get these gardens looking like they did when she lived here.'

Joanna appreciated his thoughtfulness, hoping that she could do anything in her power to help him achieve some closure. 'Fair enough. I'm sure you'll be able to get it back as good as new.'

They walked down the long driveway towards the front of the house and Joanna looked up at the old, faded weatherboards. 'It really is a beautiful old home,' she said. 'A lick of paint to tidy it up and it'd be the best on the street.'

He looked up and down the old building, remembering all the happy and sad memories he had in there, and said to Joanna, 'Someone will get the chance to make it that.'

As they reached the end of the driveway, Joanna looked at the shining black ute and then across to her police car.

'Can I drive?' she asked him, pointing at the ute.

He smiled and threw the key over in her direction. 'Of course, although it's got a little bit more power than your Landcruiser.'

Walking over towards the ute, Joanna ran her hand along the shining black bonnet. 'Always wanted one of these as a kid,' she said. 'My Dad had a similar car; me and my brother were never allowed in it.'

He remembered their conversation earlier, about her abusive childhood with her father. 'What happened to your Dad?'

'Dead. Cirrhosis of the liver. Drank himself to death, died in a nursing home,' she replied, with a sour look on her face. 'I didn't attend the funeral.'

He thought that whatever her father had done to her must have been quite bad to cause that reaction. Choosing not to extend the conversation any further, he climbed into the passenger seat. 'Try not to break it.'

'I won't,' she replied, turning the key in the ignition, giving it a couple of revs. She smiled and asked, 'Where to?'

'The petrol station.'

Nick and Joanna made their way over to the eastern side of town in the V8 ute, rumbling along the country streets. He felt like he was in a time machine, almost back in 1992 when he had lost his mother, with distant memories of her and his father driving away in the ute, while he and his sister had sleepovers at his grandmother's.

Pulling into the petrol station, he noticed a closed sign on the faded and chipped front door. 'What's that all about, I wonder?' he asked Joanna as she switched the ute off.

'Let's go and find out,' she replied.

Making their way through the old petrol bowsers and the oil-stained concrete, they walked up to the door. Knocking on it and yelling, 'Police!' they heard footsteps shuffle over to the door and keys entering the rusted locks. They both stepped back to allow the person room.

'Help you?' Julie Mason asked, squinting into the bright sunlight.

Noticing her crumpled track suit pants and tea-stained T-shirt, Joanna was the first person to speak of the two.

'Mrs Mason, it's Jo,' she said, a warm smile on her face. 'Everything ok?'

Recognition dawned on Julie's face as her eyes focused on the young senior constable. 'Hi lovely, I'm sorry,' she said, tears beginning to well in her eyes. 'It's Earl. He's in the hospital. They're saying he had a heart attack.'

Nick couldn't believe the news, after having only talked to the elderly station attendant days earlier. 'Julie, it's Nick Vada,' he said, using his height to block the sun from shining in her face. 'Is there anything we can do to help?'

Julie's eyes scanned from Joanna and over to Nick. 'Oh, Nick,' she said, beginning to cry. 'I'm sorry about your father.'

Nick smiled warmly at the elderly attendant. 'Let's not worry about my Dad right now. What can we do to help?'

'He's been transferred to Edithvale,' she said with a worried look on her face. 'Our car is at the mechanics, and we don't have anyone left. I just don't know what to do.'

Joanna walked through the doorway and gave the elderly attendant a warm hug. 'Let's get you a cup of tea Julie, then we will drive you to Edithvale,' she said, looking at Nick. 'Go and grab the Landcruiser.'

He turned on his heel and made his way back to the V8 ute, smiling as the trusty engine fired at the first turn of the key. Making his way back to the police car at his family home, he quickly ran back inside the house and grabbed the old manilla police file on the table. Returning to the petrol station, he pulled the Landcruiser up to the front door and made his way back inside. The old shop attendant and Joanna were sitting at a small dining table behind the shop counter.

After helping Julie pack a bag of clothes, Joanna helped the elderly gas station attendant into the back of the Landcruiser. 'He'll be ok Julie, he's a tough old bugger.'

Chapter Twenty-Nine

Making their way out onto the highway towards Edithvale with Nick driving, Joanna explained to him the story of how she and Julie had got to know each other through a mutual love of cooking; with the elderly petrol station attendant dropping dishes around to her home during her first weeks in town.

'She was so young, Nick,' Julie said from the back seat of the noisy Landcruiser. 'She looked like she'd just come out of school.'

'Her head looked like it barely came over that steering wheel,' she said with a hearty laugh, as she pointed to the steering wheel. 'And her first time in the petrol station in her uniform, I thought she was going to a fancy-dress party.'

Nick laughed along with her, with Joanna joining in. 'Ha-ha, very funny, I guess I looked extremely young when I got here.'

Falling into silence, Nick looked out into the vast paddocks on the outskirts of his hometown. The massive piles of grain covered in blue tarps running along the fence lines were used as a protection from birds trying to eat it. Further along the gun barrel straight highway, he sighted the white Milford police highway patrol car coming towards them in the distance.

Giving Jack a wave as the elderly highway patrolman went past, he heard Julie Mason pipe up in the back seat. 'Jack Thomson,' she swooned. 'He was a dreamboat back in the day.'

'You knew Jack when he played football?' he asked.

'He was a star,' Julie said. 'Would've made the big time if he didn't have that knee injury,' she said, referring to the gruesome knee injury Jack received during a football game in the late 80s.

'Yeah, Dad and him told me all the stories,' he said to her with a smile in the rear-view mirror. 'Heard the town was a different place back then.'

'Oh, Nick, it's hard to even describe,' Julie said, with her eyes closed as she reminisced about her glory days. 'The farmers were producing more grain than they knew what to do with. The money that poured into this town was even more than the Chinese,' she said, talking about the solar panel projects he had recently learnt all about.

'Did you know, Nick? I knew your **Mum** quite well,' Julie said in his direction. 'She helped around at the station from time to time.'

Not knowing about his mother ever having a job, he said, 'Oh, really? I never knew she worked.'

'She was great, Nick. I never had to lift a finger. Some days me and Earl could even head to Edithvale for a day out,' Julie said, with a smile on her face. 'I never trusted anyone else to run the station the way she did.'

He listened to stories of his mother's time working in the service station in Milford with a smile on his face.

'Julie,' Joanna asked. 'What do you think happened to Billie?'

The car fell into silence as Julie thought back to the time of her mother's murder. They waited with anticipation for her thoughts on the matter. 'You know, Nick, your mother was quite the looker back in the day. She was absolutely breathtaking. Your sister Jess reminds me a lot of her. She had many admirers before she met your father, Tim.'

'Dad always did say he was the luckiest man on earth.'

'He sure was. There wasn't a man in Milford who didn't try their luck there,' Julie said with a laugh.

'What about Russell Waterford?' Joanna asked, glancing over in Nick's direction.

'Russell was besotted by Billie. I actually said to Earl back in those days that they would've made a lovely couple. Earl always agreed.'

'Were they ever actually together?' Joanna pressed.

'Yes, I think they were,' Julie replied. 'I used to see them at the football club from time to time, hand in hand. Russell was close with Jack Thomson as well, come to think of it.'

He wondered why, when listening to Russell confess to his crimes, he hadn't made any more mention of his mother's death.

'He was absolutely devastated when she passed Nick. Russell Waterford actually paid for that ugly marble angel which stands over your mother's gravestone.'

'Wow, that's news to me,' he said. 'I never knew that.'

'I was a part of the funeral arrangements. Russell Waterford personally came to me and told me about his proposal. He asked me to never tell your Dad about the donation.'

His memory went back to the time during his mother's funeral; his only memories being of men and women in black coming to him and offering their condolences. And feeling the heat of the day making his little body sweat in the itchy new suit his grandmother had bought for him.

'We are so sorry for your loss,' was said, over and over again, by people he didn't quite know.

'Thank you,' he said, again and again, wondering when the day was going to end and when his **Mum** would come back.

'What about Samantha Waterford?' he asked Julie.

'She came later in the picture. She was away at boarding school and was back and forth between Milford and Sydney a fair bit. I think she was always considered a little bit of an outsider, but she tried hard to fit in.'

He struggled to think there would ever be a time in his life that Samantha Waterford would be an outsider. He tried to imagine a younger woman, unsure of herself, going back and forth between country and city, trying to fit in with the cliques and social circles in both places, trying to pretend to be something that she wasn't.

'It all sort of happened quickly,' Julie continued. 'Billie was originally from Edithvale and your Dad was away a lot with work and they met at the local show. With his Akubra always on and blue singlet on his back, I think Billie got swept away by the bushman. She fell head over heels for your Dad and that was that.'

He smiled at the thought of his parents in the past. Driving around town in the ute and enjoying local football matches. A simpler time.

'I think Russell Waterford was hurt when he came back from Vietnam. Tim was in the picture and then it seemed like he and Samantha got together, and the rest is history.'

Nick thought of Milford's power couple, Russell and Samantha Waterford, owners of the biggest farm in the district and living at Warranilla, in the beautiful homestead.

'Warranilla was a dump back then,' Julie continued. 'Samantha commissioned massive renovations.'

His memories were not as clear of the old homestead back from when his father would take him out shooting. They mostly scouted the paddocks toward the wide and dark green sections of the river which snaked throughout the property.

'The Waterford family actually lived in a small house out towards the east sheds. Once the renovations were completed, Samantha moved the elderly Waterfords, Russell's **Mum** and Dad, Jenny and Jack into Edithvale and into a retirement home.'

Nick thought of her shipping the elderly Waterfords off to a retirement home after their years spent on the land, growing crops, and raising their family. 'Quite cruel,' he replied. 'I've never seen that side of Samantha.'

'She's very different these days,' Julie said. 'The fake English accent has certainly made her seem a lot more refined than she was back in those days.'

The trio fell silent once again as Nick saw the outline of Edithvale coming into view. 'To the Edithvale hospital?' he asked.

'Yes, thank you Nick.'

Pulling into the hospital, Joanna and Nick got out of the police Landcruiser. Helping Julie with her bags and into the entrance of the hospital, Julie turned back to him and said, 'You know what, Nick? I really don't think Jim Hooper had anything to do with your Mum's murder. I know that's what a lot of people thought back then. I think it was someone in town. Thanks so much for the lift, I appreciate it.'

He watched the elderly fuel station attendant walk slowly into the hospital and was once again left with more questions in his head than answers.

Joanna walked slowly back to the police Landcruiser with the keys in hand. 'So, sounds like you learnt a few things on the drive.'

'Yeah, I did,' he replied. 'Why do I feel like Russell Waterford has more to do with my mother's murder than he ever wanted to admit?'

His mind raced with thoughts of the night in the east sheds, with Russell Waterford waving the knife in his hand with a mad look in his eyes. He winced slightly as he looked down at his right arm in the sling. With the painkillers starting to wear off, he could feel his head beginning to thump. 'I think we should go and talk with Russell Waterford.'

'Ok,' Joanna replied. 'He's been transferred here to the Edithvale lockup. Let's go while we're in town.'

Making the drive through the river town and towards the police station, he looked at the full streets, with tourist buses lining the carparks, and most of the small shops full to the brim. 'It's a shame Milford never really went the way of Edithvale,' he said to Joanna.

'Milford has its own special bit of charm, though, doesn't it? I just don't like all these crowds.'

'It's certainly a special place,' he said, as he thought of Jemma and all his great childhood memories back in his small hometown.

Pulling up out the front of the large police station, they marvelled at the size of the building. Shiny blue tiles adorned the façade, with floor to ceiling dark tinted commercial windows spanning the front of the building. 'Edithvale Police Station' was written on a small red gum sign which was framed by the blue tiles.

'Looks like the money ran out at Edithvale,' he said, thinking of the tiny ramshackle police station back at Milford.

'I agree,' Joanna laughed, eyes spanning the huge glass expanse of a building. 'Let's go.'

The two officers walked through the automatic front doors and felt the cool air blowing down the back of their shirts. Standing inside a huge entrance, Nick looked over at all the posters adorning the walls, from news articles celebrating the works of the local cops, through to Neighbourhood Watch advertisements.

All stations are really the same, he thought to himself, picturing his station back in Sydney where some of his first few years as a constable were spent manning the front desk. Domestic disputes and lost pets being the hardest part of his day.

'Help you?' said the curt professional voice of the constable manning the front counter, his short buzz cut and neatly ironed shirt displaying a military-like precision.

'Detective **Sergeant** Vada and Senior Constable Joanna Gray,' he said to the young constable, flashing his police badge. 'Hoping to speak with your Inspector in charge.'

Recognition dawned on the young constable's face, with his eyebrows rising as he heard Nick's name. 'Afternoon, **Sergeant**,' he replied, ignoring Joanna's introduction. 'Shit mate, you're a hero around here. We heard you had been stood down when you caught Russell Waterford? What a badass,' he said with a chuckle.

'Just doing my job,' he said to the young officer sheepishly, looking in Joanna's direction. 'The Inspector?'

The young constable composed himself. 'Shit, sorry, through the double doors and to the left.'

Nick and Joanna made their way through the double doors and into the impressive, brand-new police station. Long rows of desks with state-of-the-art computers lined the walls of the building, with the floor-to-ceiling windows at the front filling the room with cascading beams of sunlight.

Making their way down the hallway with the young constable, he pointed to the last glass windowed office in the corner of the building. 'Inspector Greg Baseley,' he said.

Eyes widening at the sight of Nick and Joanna, the Inspector waved them in with a smile. 'Good afternoon, Detective Vada,' he said, introducing himself. 'Inspector Greg Baseley,' he continued, pointing at the nameplate on the door. 'And you must be Senior Constable Joanna Gray?' he said in Joanna's direction. 'I personally helped sign off on your promotion. When Jim called and ran through what happened at Warranilla, I thought it well deserved.'

Joanna smiled at the Inspector. In his early 60s, he had a commanding presence with neatly trimmed grey hair, black-framed glasses covering brilliant blue eyes and an impressive tan.

'How's the body Nick?' the Inspector asked, looking at his sling.

'I'll live.'

'Your work was crucial in apprehending a prolific serial killer. Contrary to what people might say, I believe Russell Waterford had developed a taste for it. And would've killed again.'

'Russell Waterford is actually the reason why we are here,' he said to the Inspector. 'I'd like the opportunity to talk to him, if possible.'

'I see no reason why you shouldn't get that chance, detective. And why would you like to do that?'

'It's about my mother, sir.'

Nick didn't particularly feel like talking about her, but knew this may be his only chance to talk to Russell Waterford. 'She was murdered in 1992, and I believe he may have done it. It's been in the back of my mind ever since I got to Milford. There is something there sir, I can feel it.'

The Inspector's smile faded as he thought back to his earlier days on the force. 'Yes, Billie Vada? I remember it like it was yesterday. You don't get many murders in this area, and it was basically all Jim Hooper back then.'

The name Jim Hooper made Nick's skin crawl as he thought back to the serial killer. 'Do you think he had anything to do with it?'

The Inspector leant back in his chair and put his hands on top of his head, deep in thought. 'Look, I worked with Detective Jason Peters on and off during those times. And we actually discussed your mother's case quite a lot. Jason was convinced it was Hooper for a time and then he wasn't so sure. He actually still lives in Edithvale. I'm sure he'd love a visit and a chance to reminisce?'

Nick couldn't believe his luck; the chance to talk to the man who had written most of the report that he had carried and obsessed over for most of his policing career. 'I thought he had moved to Queensland?'

'Yeah, he did; lasted about a month,' the Inspector said with a laugh. 'I think he played three rounds of golf and missed the country life too much. He's actually doing a small amount of private investigation work for the right people.'

'Well, that's great news,' Joanna added. 'We will definitely go and see him.'

'I'll give you his number and let him know you guys are in town. Now, Russell Waterford, we'll get him into interview room four.'

Nick relished the chance to speak with the elderly landowner again.

Chapter Thirty

Escorting them back towards the main entrance, the Inspector directed them toward a large staircase to the right of the double doors. 'Upstairs and to the right, I hope you get some answers, detective.'

'Appreciate it,' he replied, already beginning to make his way up the stairs.

As they ascended the wide staircase, he felt the dull pain in his leg begin to get worse, and realised he was starting to sweat slightly. Joanna noticed a change in the detective and spoke first. 'You okay, Nick?' she asked, worried about his sudden change in demeanour.

'Yeah, I'm fine,' he said, trying to remain cool. 'Let's try to get some answers.'

As they approached the door at the end of the hallway, he spoke to Joanna.

'Let me take the lead,' he said, with Joanna replying with a curt nod.

Looking into the brand-new state-of-the-art interview room, he saw the elderly landowner sitting at a white desk, with his hands pressed together in handcuffs, connected to the bench. In a dark blue cotton top and bottoms, he looked over and through the clear interview room window towards Nick and Joanna and smiled in their direction.

'He looks happy to see us,' she said with a chuckle.

'Yeah, I bet.'

Opening the solid interview room door, they got the chance to look at Russell Waterford up close. The once commanding landowner of half of Milford now seemed a shadow of his former self, with the prison uniform making him look like any normal man.

Deciding to make the first move, Nick spoke. 'Afternoon Russell.'

'Nick, Joanna,' Russell said to the two officers. 'Nice to see some familiar faces.'

Nick, not in the mood for talking pleasantries, decided to cut to the chase. 'Russell, I'm not here to discuss your case.'

'Or your capture,' Joanna added.

The elderly landowner looked disappointed. 'Then what are you here for?'

'I want to discuss my mother's murder,' he said, getting to the point.

'I already told you, Nick, I had nothing to do with that,' he said, shaking his head. His hand instinctively reached up to scratch his head, and he looked at the cuffs and cursed, 'Fuckin' things.'

'Do you have any idea what happened to my mother?'

'I loved her, Nick,' Russell said, shocking him with his honesty. Was he about to finally get the confession he thought he was going to get in the east sheds?

'So, did I Russell, and my Dad and Jess did as well,' he said, wanting Russell to know the full extent of the pain he had caused.

'I loved her from the first moment I saw her. She was a few years younger than me but I always told my mates that she would be my girl one day.'

Nick was shocked, now learning the extent of their relationship. He'd always believed his mother and father to have been each other's first loves.   .

'So, what happened? Joanna asked, cutting Russell short.

'Tim Vada happened,' Russell said, almost spitting at his father's name. 'Showed up and swept her off her feet. I never stood a chance.'

'Well, if she loved you so much, why did she go with my father?'

'Who knows? Flash ute, heaps of cash from shearing, beats me. But I got home from Vietnam and the minute Tim turned up, I was old news.' The elderly landowner looked down at his hands. 'I was heir to the biggest piece of land in the state and half the shops in town and your Dad took her away from me.'

Nick, frustrated at Russell talking about his mother like she was some prize, was beginning to get irritated. 'So how did you meet Samantha?'

'Sam…' Russell frowned. 'She was always around, but nothing compared to your mother. I never loved her the way I loved your mother,' Russell said, looking into his eyes. 'She was horribly jealous of Billie; I think she knew that I would always love her.'

'So why did you kill mum then!?' he said, struggling to keep his voice down, knowing that the Inspector would've been listening in on the interview.

'Nick, I swear to you, I never had anything to do with your mother's death. When I found out she had been murdered, I was devastated. I didn't sleep for a week.' He looked down at his handcuffed hands again. 'I still miss her every day.'

Nick sat in the cold meeting room, unable to understand what was happening. His train of thought had been turned upside down.

'When she passed, I was a mess. I felt so sorry for your family. I even let your Dad work on Warranilla from time to time. And I even let you and him shoot on the property. I just couldn't stand to see him near the homestead though, the loss of Billie was too much.' That explained his foggy memory of the property before the renovations, Nick thought.

Joanna cut in. 'So, what do *you* think happened to Billie Vada?'

Russell sighed and looked at both of them one by one. 'I genuinely don't know.'

Sitting quietly for what felt like five minutes, Nick cut through the silence. 'Do you have any more thoughts, Russell? Because we have places to be,' he said, as he began to make the move to get up out of his chair.

'No, wait. I've thought about it a lot, actually. Jim Hooper actually spent time working at Warranilla on and off during the time your mother was murdered.'

Nick couldn't believe what he had just heard, confirming his belief that the notorious serial killer had been in the region during the time of his mother's murder. 'And you didn't think this information was of interest to the police?' he said angrily. 'They could've drilled him for it, Russell.'

'Nick, I was devastated when your mother passed, but he was just another worker in a cast of thousands who have worked my farms over the years. It was actually Samantha who reminded me he worked on the farm. She remembered him causing trouble in town back then.'

Nick thought back to the stories he had heard about him bashing the local footballer in town. 'Is there anything else you can tell me?'

'I thought it was your Dad for a while, truly,' he said, looking him in the eyes. 'But I was close friends with Gary Jones, and he swore black and blue that Tim was with him for that whole night.'

'It wasn't my Dad,' he said, feeling the anger beginning to rise. 'He would never do that to my mother.'

'I think that's enough for today,' Joanna said, cutting off the conversation, sensing his anger. 'Thank you for your time, Russell.'

The elderly landowner fell silent once again. Looking down at his handcuffed hands, he looked up at Nick one last time. 'Please Nick, can you speak to Pete? I want to talk to him; I want to see my son.'

'That's not up to me,' Nick said with finality. 'Goodbye Russell.'

The two officers walked out of the meeting room and down the long hallway, pausing at the top of the stairs as sunshine streamed through the floor to ceiling windows. 'Thank you,' was all he could say to Joanna.

'It's ok, I know how hard all of this must be for you bringing up all of these old wounds.'

He said nothing as they made their way down the staircase and into the expansive office space. The Inspector approached. 'So, what do you think?'

Nick sighed, frustration evident in his voice, 'I think he's telling the truth; I believe him.'

The Inspector looked at Nick. 'Don't let it get you down son, you have multiple avenues to continue down.'

'Yes, I think our number one suspect is now Jim Hooper,' Joanna said.

'With the number of women he killed, it's certainly a high possibility,' the Inspector said.

Nick's mind raced with memories of flashing lights, crunching gravel, and muffled voices in the night. Could it be that simple? Was his mother just another one of Hooper's victims? It just didn't seem to fit.

The Inspector added, 'I gave Jason Peters your number Nick, I'm sure you will hear from him.'

'Thankyou.'

Walking out of the station, he felt once again like he had more questions rather than answers. Were Russell Waterford and his mother truly a couple, as Russell had described? And why hadn't his father discussed it with him? Embarrassment being the main reason, Nick assumed.

As they got into Joanna's Landcruiser, he heard his phone ring in his pocket. 'Detective Vada speaking.'

'Nick, Jason Peters here, heard from Greg Baseley just now that you wanted to have a chat?'

'Yes, Mr. Peters, we are actually in Edithvale as we speak. I know it's getting late. Any chance we could come for a quick chat?'

'Call me Jason, mate,' he replied, putting the two on a first name basis. 'Of course, who couldn't pass up an opportunity to talk about the past? Shall we have dinner? The Edithvale Hotel, 7pm.'

He couldn't believe his luck, after the time wasted talking to Russell Waterford. 'Sounds good Jason, we will see you there.'

He hung up the phone, and Joanna looked at him expectantly.

'Looks like we have a dinner date,' he replied, looking at his watch. 'In an hour,' he added.

'With Jason Peters?' Joanna had a smile on her face. 'What an opportunity.'

Chapter Thirty-One

With the sun beginning to set in the river town, Nick and Joanna made their way toward the Edithvale Hotel. Built in 1883, it was the biggest building in the region for many years. Upon completion, it was opened by a minister from Sydney, and when he remarked that it looked like an establishment that could belong in Sydney, further research was made into the funding and construction of the building. It turned out that a prominent architect in Sydney had incorrectly marked drawings set for a grand hotel being built in Sydney, and had shipped them accidentally to Edithvale. With construction three quarters complete on the massive structure, the architect was made aware of the mistake and decided to let it remain, and so it became a grand tourist attraction in the region for many years to come.

Parking near the entrance and getting out of their car, Nick and Joanna marvelled at the beautiful two storey building. Set on the corner facing the main roundabout in the centre of the township, it dwarfed the other buildings around it. With a white colonial facade and feature mouldings, its wide columns supported a full top floor veranda. The place heaved with live music, and he hoped that they could find a quiet place to have a word with the detective.

'Impressive, isn't it?' he said, having relayed the story of the hotel's construction to his young partner on the drive over.

'It certainly is,' she remarked. 'Definitely looks like it belongs in Sydney and not in Edithvale.'

'Let's hope we find a place quiet to talk,' he said as they walked up to the entrance of the grand old pub. Looking in through the doors at the bustling crowd of patrons, with a live acoustic act in the corner, Nick worried that the old detective may not want to indulge too much information out in public.

Walking in through the doors and over to the main bar, he asked the barman for the directions to the dining area.

'Door on your right mate, right down past the gaming room and to the left,' the barman yelled to them, while drying out a freshly cleaned pot glass.

They made their way down the long hallway and came to a doorway to the left, walking out into a newly renovated, huge outdoor dining area. A massive expanse of red gum decking had neat tables and chairs spread across the vast area.

'Must be money in Edithvale,' Joanna exclaimed.

'I agree.'

'I came here as a kid with my Dad and sister, but it was nothing like this when I was here,' he said, with memories of dark smoke-filled rooms full of men in blue singlets and work shirts. 'It's certainly a lot nicer these days.'

Sitting over towards the corner of the expansive deck and waving in their direction was Detective Jason Peters. A now bald, thinly-built man with dark glasses and a silver moustache, Nick couldn't help but think he looked like an older version of Edithvale's Inspector.

Heading over in Jason's direction, Nick was pleased to be away from the heaving pub crowd and noise of the front bar. 'Detective Nick Vada and Senior Constable Joanna Gray,' Nick said, introducing themselves to the legendary detective.

'Pleasure to meet you both,' he replied, shaking Joanna's hand and then his. He was surprised by the firmness of the elderly man's grip.

'Read about your work up in Sydney, Nick, a fine job,' Jason added, referring to a previous case in Sydney. 'And of course, heard all about your exploits in Milford from Greg.'

'Thank you, we appreciate it,' Joanna replied.

'You're very welcome. Now, seems like you would like to talk about the past. I am guessing you would like to discuss your mother's case, Nick?'

He had often dreamt of the day he could discuss specifics with the detective who had been the lead on his mother's case, and with so many things running through his mind, he wasn't sure where to start.

Jason, sensing his unease, decided for him. 'Billie Vada, 34 years old, found deceased in her bedroom, in your family home,' the detective said, looking in his direction. 'No signs of forced entry, evidence of an argument and a small scuffle in the dining room. She had multiple stab wounds in her chest, and one hit her heart, causing her to bleed out.'

Hearing the gruesome details of his mother's death out loud caused Nick to pause. Was he doing the right thing in bringing up the past like this? He had just lost his father and hadn't given himself any time to grieve. Joanna was the first to break the silence.

'Any witnesses?' she asked.

'None. I personally spoke with you that day, Nick. You were so young, 7 years old, you couldn't really tell us much, just that you had heard a car and muffled voices.'

He was surprised at hearing this. He had never been sure whether he had spoken with the detectives and had no memory of it. 'I have the case file from the investigation,' he said.

'You may have the Milford copy that was in the records,' Jason said, pulling a similar but much thicker folder out of a small leather briefcase he had down by his feet. 'This is my personal case file for the murder.'

Nick's eyes widened.

'It's yours,' Jason said, sliding the file over the table to him. 'I have my own copies, of course.'

'Thank you, Jason,' he said, looking at the file like it was a lost piece of treasure.

'No problem at all, son.'

Joanna got up and went to get a round of drinks and order dinner, with the elderly detective recommending the steak.

'Three steaks it is then,' Joanna replied, walking off.

'So, do you think Jim Hooper killed my mother?' he asked.

'Yes, and no,' Jason replied. 'Hooper's victims were more often than not viciously bashed.' The elderly detective looked down and rubbed his face. 'I've seen things that you wouldn't believe Nick, such brutality, and also he sexually assaulted most victims, with break and enter being his main method of entry into the house.'

'We spoke with Russell Waterford today, and he told us that Jim Hooper had been shearing on Warranilla on or around the time of my mother's murder.'

'Hmmm I see,' the detective replied, lost in thought. 'We did in the end strike him off the official suspect list. Looking at the timeline, your mother would've been his second last victim, and his final victim, Carlie Manning's murder, was actually eerily similar to your mother's Nick. No break and enter, no sexual assault and she was viciously stabbed to death.'

'Maybe he was changing his pattern?' Joanna asked as she returned to the table.

'It is certainly a possibility, and it's something I have seen before. I am just thankful we finally caught him when we did, and it was all thanks to DNA, certainly made my job a lot easier.'

'So, do you have any other theories?' he asked.

'Potentially someone she knew, but no one we interviewed had any reason to kill her, and she had no enemies, so once your father's alibi was confirmed, we were really lost for answers.'

The biggest problem with the known assailant theory, was that it was based on the detective's thinking that his mother would've opened the screen and front door to welcome the killer into the home, but Nick knew that their home was open at all times for any person to come and go as they pleased.

A young woman in her twenties with a high blonde ponytail, an 'Edithvale Hotel' apron, and a warm smile lowered three huge plates of Scotch fillet steak and mashed potatoes down onto the table in front of them. Nick realised he hadn't eaten since breakfast, and all three made quick work of the beautiful pub food in front of them. Draining his beer glass, the detective wiped his mouth and looked over toward him. 'So, what do you think, Nick?' The elderly detective asked him the question he had had on his mind for the past 31 years of his life.

'I think Jim Hooper killed my mother,' he said with finality.

'Well, there is one way to truly find out.'

'And what's that?'

'We still have crime scene samples with unknown DNA in the state archives. Because the case was never put under Jim

Hooper's list of victims, we never tested his DNA against the skin particles found on the edge of your dining table.'

He felt the air leave his lungs. Obviously not included in the Milford case file, Nick never knew that any forensic samples were taken at the crime scene at his home. 'They actually took samples?' he asked, shocked.

'Yes, we did.'

'Well, why didn't you test them?'

Jason let out a long sigh. 'Nick, I may have caught many killers in my career, but there are still many unanswered questions left. My time in the force is done,' he said, looking him in the eyes. 'It's your time to get some answers.'

Nick knew that in his position; it was simply a request for evidence and a quick email to DNA testing and he could finally have the answer to his mother's murder from 30 years earlier. 'I didn't know that,' he said, unable to find the words to speak, with his mind racing a million miles an hour.

'We've got him,' Joanna replied to Nick with a smile.

Chapter Thirty-Two

Nick's mind raced with all the possibilities before him as they made the drive back to Milford. A quiet anticipation buzzed through the silent car with the 100km drive feeling like it only took five minutes.

Joanna dropped him back at his house on Evans Street and waved him goodbye, both of them hoping for good news to come from the impending DNA tests.

He walked back in the front yard and over to the side tap, and turned the sprinkler off, hoping that the good drenching put a little bit of life back into his new lawn.

Walking through the front door, he slowly traced the likely steps that he believed Jim Hooper took on that fateful night. Silently down the hallway past his and Jess's bedroom doors, and onwards down to the dining room, imagining the light footsteps he would've walked.

Coming into the dining room, he imagined that his mother must have got up to get something from the kitchen, perhaps a wine, while she watched a movie in the lounge room. Picturing her face wide with shock at seeing a stranger in the dining room, he lunges at her, pushing over the dining chair in his way. Scraping his hip hard on the dining table, he feels warm blood seep from the wound underneath his shorts. She manages to scratch him badly on the neck and he pushes her as hard as he possibly can through the kitchen doorway, with one of her hands grabbing the left-hand architrave, causing deep scratch marks.

As she screams, 'No, no, please! My children!' Jim picks her up off the ground with one arm and carries her into her bedroom, lying her on the bed one hand held tightly over her throat, causing her to not make a sound. He removes a knife from the sheath clipped to his belt and swiftly stabs her again and again with a deep satisfaction, the urge to kill overpowering everything else.

Watching the life seep slowly from her eyes, he notices her diamond wedding ring glistening in the bedroom light. Never taking a souvenir before, he decides he just might this time and pockets it. As the blood now pools at the base of the bed, he decides his work is done, and traipses bloody footprints straight out of the hallway and back the way he came.

Now standing at the foot of his father's bed, snapping back to the present, Nick felt his head begin to ache. He needed answers, and he knew he was close to getting them. Walking back towards the fridge in the dimly lit kitchen, he grabbed a cold beer and made his way onto the couch. Finishing only two mouthfuls, he slowly drifted off into a deep sleep, exhausted from the long day.

The next morning at the local police station, Nick sat next to Joanna in quiet anticipation as she typed out the email to the state record archives. Marked URGENT, she requested DNA information pertaining to the cold case for the murder of Billie Vada, to be tested against samples obtained from inmate number 723809 of Goulburn supermax prison, Jim Hooper.

As she clicked send, Nick felt relief wash over him, knowing he would receive a call within 24 hours indicating whether it was a match. He felt like he had his answers so close in front of him that he could almost smell it. Joanna broke the silence, 'I can't believe we may already have answers,' she said. 'It's only been a few days.'

'It may have only been a day for you,' Nick said, as he looked down towards the file on the desk. 'But I've been at this nearly my whole life.'

'Well, I hope you find some answers finally, Nick. You deserve it.'

'Thank you.'

After sitting and discussing Russell Waterford's confession and capture at the farm with the Sarge and Joanna while drinking the station's bitter instant coffee, he decided he had better go suit shopping for the upcoming wedding. Through text messages, his sister had kept him up to date on the wedding plans, advising him that Samantha, after a rough couple of days, had taken Russell's arrest in her stride and had completely moved her focus onto the wedding. Moving the location to Warranilla, she had hired a catering company and band from Sydney at short notice, costing a small fortune.

'I think it's good for her focus to be elsewhere,' his sister had typed out. 'She needs this right now. After everything that has happened, the deaths and with Dad passing, she wants this wedding to be a fresh start.'

He had wondered how the elderly Waterford matriarch would manage without her husband, as they had been so close, and he also wondered whether she would be interested in talking to him about his mother, considering he now knew that they had known each other more intimately than he had realised. Possibly even competing for Russell's affection for a short period.

Heading into Revells, he was surprised to see two more people inside the shop trying on clothes. Busy day, he thought to himself with a smile, happy that Jemma's shop finally had a few customers. He made his way over to the suit section again after deciding to not wear the same suit from the funeral again, he hoped to find a nicer casual jacket than the old one he had bought with him from Sydney, and he also wanted to secretly prop up Jemma's business.

After helping the two customers with their purchases and walking them to the door, Jemma turned around, looking back at him. 'I wish we would have big weddings in town more often,' she laughed. 'This is the busiest I've been in months.'

Years more like it, he thought quietly to himself, as he looked over at the dated and dusty mannequins. 'I'm glad you're busy.'

'How are you feeling?' she asked, looking at his sling with her eyes full of worry.

'I'm ok,' he said. 'Might be time to get rid of this sling.'

He filled Jemma in on his interview with Russell Waterford, his chat with Jason Peters, and the submission of the serial killer's DNA.

On hearing of the submission of Jim Hooper's DNA results, Jemma's eyes widened. 'Oh, Nick, I can't believe it. You may finally have answers!'

'I hope so.'

After trying on a few jackets with Jemma's help, he settled on a dark grey western style jacket from Country Road, which was the most expensive he could find, and a matching pair of neat chinos completed with a new belt.

'I know what you're doing,' she said, smiling at him as she ran up the amount on her outdated shop till. 'That'll be $650.'

Supporting local businesses, he thought to himself as he gladly tapped his credit card on Jemma's EFTPOS machine. 'I'd rather spend it here than in the city,' he replied as he put his card back into his wallet. 'Now one more question,' he said, quite sure of the answer.

'Yes?'

'Want to come to a wedding?'

'Thought you'd never ask.'

His phone rang at that moment. Pulling the mobile out of his pocket with his left hand and seeing an unknown number, he wondered if the DNA results could be back so soon? It had only been a few hours.

'Detective Sergeant Nick Vada.'

'Good afternoon detective, this is Gabby Hodges of the NSW Forensic Biology and DNA Analysis lab. How are you today?'

Feeling time slowing down, he held his phone in a vice-like grip. Unable to grasp the possibility that he could be just about to solve his mother's murder, he replied, 'I'm fine, thank you; do you have the results of my request?'

He heard papers being flipped in the background as the scientist read out the freshly printed report.

'Yes, we do,' she said, as time stood still, and he felt like they were the only two people in the world at that moment.

'DNA results from inmate 723809 are not a match for your sample.'

Chapter Thirty-Three

Nick hung up the phone and stood in the middle of the shop in silence, not being able to even say thank you to the scientist. He felt his world crashing down around him. If Jim Hooper didn't kill his mother, then who did? There weren't many serial killers in Australia and it was just way too convenient that one had been in and around his hometown during his mother's murder.

He looked down at the blank phone screen. Jemma, sensing his frustration, asked, 'Good news?'

'No,' he replied, putting his phone back in his pocket. 'Not good news. It's not a match.'

'I don't understand. You seemed so sure?'

'I really was,' he said with a sigh, wondering how he could've been so wrong. What had his years of training been for?

If he or Jason Peters couldn't get to the bottom of this, no one could. 'I need to speak with Joanna. I'm sorry I've got to go. I will pick you up tomorrow for the wedding.'

'Okay,' Jemma replied.

He walked out of the shop with his clothes in hand, breathing in the warm, still air. He felt the same unmistakable tingle on the end of his tongue, and he knew in that moment, all he needed was a drink.

Walking back to the old ute, he threw the bags into the back tray and walked over to the Coachman's Inn diagonally across the road. Walking straight through the front door and up to the bar, he looked over at Marty polishing a glass while chatting with one of the bar flies at the end of the bar and spoke, 'Can I get a takeaway?'

'Of course, mate. What are you after?'

He pointed under the bar at the cheapest Russian vodka he had on the shelf. 'That.' Was all he could manage to say.

Marty's eyebrows rose slightly, and he looked long and hard at Nick. 'You alright, mate?'

He wasn't in the mood for pleasantries. 'I'm fine,' he replied, grabbing the bottle off Marty, and throwing a fifty-dollar note on the bar. 'Keep the change.'

Making his way down to the river, he found a quiet park bench to sit on. Cracking the red lid off the cheap bottle, he tipped it back and poured it in, and felt the liquid, hot and burning down his throat.

Who the hell killed my mother and why? he thought to himself, as he drank. Did my father have something to do with it? Is Russell Waterford still lying to me? What more can I do? He wondered, staring at the dark green river, with the water slowly moving against the upturned gumtrees that had tipped into the river after years of erosion. Why was he even still here, and what was the point? he thought, as he felt the vodka mixing with his strong painkillers and beginning to make his head swim.

Continuing to take massive gulps from the clear bottle, he didn't really care what would happen to him anymore and wondered whether he should just quit the force, and live in his childhood home, with death eventually coming to his door like it did for his father and mother. As the warm sun began to fade from behind the river gums, he lay down on the bench and decided to rest his eyes, and soon, the painkillers knocked him out. His dreams were full of blood-stained hallways and walls, and he heard his mother's screams over and over.

'Shit Nick, get up,' came a voice from up above him.

Opening his eyes slightly and seeing nothing, he felt like his head had been hit by a sledgehammer. 'Whadddyawant?' he slurred.

As hands grabbed his shirt and pull him up, he felt an uncontrollable urge to vomit, and he unloaded the contents of his stomach directly over Pete Waterford's neat polo T-shirt.

'Jesus Christ Nick! What the hell!' Pete screamed, dropping him and jumping back. 'That's fucking gross!'

Nick's eyes shot open, and he realised he had fallen asleep on the park bench down by the river. Feeling his face go red with embarrassment, he looked over towards his future brother-in-law who was wearing vomit all over his shirt. Wiping his wet mouth with the back of his hand, he finally spoke, 'God, I'm so sorry Pete,' he said, looking up at the sun blaring high in the sky. 'What time is it?'

Pete stood in the hot sun looking down at him, and shook his head. 'It's 12, Nick. Jess has been worried sick about you. We have been searching all over the place for you.'

He couldn't believe how stupid he had been, constantly self-sabotaging and nearly ruining his sister's wedding day. 'I'm sorry Pete, you go.'

'It's not the first time,' he smirked back at Nick.

'Very funny.'

He waved Pete back to his Waterford Grain work ute.

Making his way back up the steep riverbank and hurrying back to Revells, he pulled his almost flat phone out of his pocket. With missed calls from nearly all the people he loved, he made his first call to Joanna. 'Hi Jo.'

'Nick! Everyone's been out looking for you! Where are you?' she yelled into the speaker.

'I'm fine, I just needed some time to myself,' he replied, choosing not to go into specifics about his night spent on the park bench.

'I know,' Joanna said, sensing what he was going to say before he said it. 'The DNA results came back; Jim Hooper didn't kill your Mum,' she said.

'We will find who did this, Nick,' she continued. 'If it's the last thing we do.'

'Thanks Jo, I really think we will,' he finally answered, deciding that after the wedding he was going to sort out his problems and get to the bottom of everything once and for all.

'Now go and enjoy your wedding. I'll talk to you tomorrow.'

He hung up the phone and made his way to the back of Revells and up the stairs of Jemma's small apartment. Lightly tapping on the rear door, it opened almost immediately. Standing inside the door was Jemma wearing a beautiful champagne-coloured slip dress, with the colour shimmering in the sunlight of the open door. Looking at her face, he could see she had been crying, despite her beautifully done makeup.

'Nick! Where the hell have you been? I was worried sick!' She yelled in his direction, tilting her face upwards, hoping her tears wouldn't ruin her makeup.

'I'm so sorry Jemma,' he replied sheepishly, embarrassed at his actions, he added, 'I just needed some space.'

She wiped the tears gently from her darkly shadowed eyes.

'Me and Jo spent half the night driving around trying to find you. I thought you might have left,' she said finally, as her tears began to slow.

He tried his best to smile and looked her up and down. 'I'm not going anywhere. Now, I need a quick shower; we have a wedding to attend.'

Jemma shook her head and walked back into the small apartment, grabbing a grey towel from the linen closet. 'Don't be long,' she said, throwing the towel in his direction.

Chapter Thirty-Four

Racing down the highway in his old ute, as the sun began to set with the orange light flickering across the dark bonnet, Nick had to smile at himself over the few days he had had. From interviewing Russell Waterford and learning of his love for his mother; his chat with Jason Peters, and learning of a second file on his mother's case with unseen DNA samples; all the way up to learning those samples were not a match and his self-destructive night spent sleeping in a park. What a ride it had been, he thought to himself, unsure whether his few weeks in Milford could ever be topped in his policing career again.

'I'm glad you're here,' Jemma smiled across at him with her hand resting on his leg. 'You've been the breath of fresh air in my life that I really think I needed.'

'I'm glad I'm here too.'

As the ute began to slow coming up to the gates of Warranilla, they fell into a comfortable silence, and he felt at peace knowing he was with one of the first loves in his life, and he was about to watch his sister get married. Not really caring at that exact moment what would happen with his Mum's case.

'It's beautiful,' Joanna said, marvelling at the massive red brick walls lining each side of the driveway entrance. The bare wrought-iron gates were open, welcoming the guests in a steady procession of cars, making their way down the gum tree-lined driveway.

'Have you ever been here before?' he asked, realising she may not have been.

'No,' she replied. 'I've heard so much about it, though.'

'It truly is a beautiful place,' he said, turning his ute into the recently slashed paddock that had neatly been turned into a car park.

Switching the keys off in the ignition, he turned to his beautiful partner, fairly sure there wasn't another woman in the world who looked better at that time. 'You ready?' he asked, grinning.

'Ready.'

The couple got out of the ute and met at the end of the tray with Nick interlocking his fingers in Jemma's. Nodding at other couples who were beginning to congregate near the white picket fence of the front yard, he felt his phone ringing in his pocket.

'Excuse me,' he said to Jemma, noticing the bride was calling.

'Hi Nick, saw Dad's ute coming down the driveway. Can you come up to the homestead?'

Unsure of why he'd be needed up there, he replied, 'Of course, sis, I'll see you shortly.'

Turning to Jemma, he saw her eyebrows raised with a questioning look.

'Jess wants me up at the homestead. Give me 5?'

'Of course,' she said, already turning to make friends with the guests mingling around them, sipping beer and wine.

He made his way through the guests, recognising many local faces as he walked, and realised that with his father's death, he had only one living family member left. With all grandparents gone and his parents having no siblings, he and Jess were the last living Vadas, and with him needing to have kids in order to continue the family name, he thought to himself.

Through the picket gates, he saw a beautiful scene. The vintage red clinker bricks were the aisle and the altar was directly in front of Warranilla's entrance, with a beautiful white arbour wrapped in jasmine flowers finishing off the scene. Crisp white chairs adorned each side of the path on the beautifully manicured grass, and the whole perimeter lined with fully bloomed camellia bushes. Gum trees loomed overhead, casting a beautiful shadow over the front yard as the sun went down. He noticed festoon lights had been hung over the whole area in preparation for the night-time nuptials.

Making his way down the aisle and up onto the front deck, he saw Pete walking out of the front door in a crisp black dinner suit, white dress shirt with bowtie, and patent leather shoes. He had never seen the farmer look so sharp in his life.

Grinning at the man for what he probably thought was one of the first times in his life, he said to his future brother-in-law, 'Looking a bit cleaner than earlier.'

Pete laughed at him. 'Yeah, I probably feel a bit better than you do right now.'

Having vomited out most of the remnants of the cheap Russian vodka, and not taking any more painkillers today, Nick actually felt clearer than he had in the last couple of weeks. 'I'll be fine mate,' he held out his hand. 'Good luck.'

Pete looked down at his hand and instead of taking it, came in and gave him a hug.

'Thanks mate,' he said. 'For everything.'

Watching Pete walk off down the end of the aisle to find his groomsmen, he made his way into the homestead down the long hallway, thinking about how much had changed since his first visit to the homestead to talk to Russell Waterford.

'In here, Nick,' came Jess's voice from inside the Waterford's master bedroom off the left-hand side of the dining room.

Walking into the massive master bedroom, he saw what looked like the biggest bed he had ever seen; the headboard carved out of solid red gum and bearing the word, Warranilla, in the centre of the headboard.

'A wedding present from Russell's mother and father,' a very stressed Samantha Waterford replied, watching his gaze fall on the gigantic bed.

'Certainly, wouldn't fit in my place,' he said with a laugh, looking at the frazzled homestead owner. Sensing her stress, he asked, 'Are you ok?'

'No!' she replied, looking on the edge of a nervous breakdown. 'One of the generators has already broken and the caterers have forgotten the duck! They've only brought lamb! What will people think?'

'It will all be completely fine,' Jess replied, walking out of the Waterford dressing room.

Wearing a stunning off-white wedding gown with intricate lace sleeves, he couldn't believe how beautiful and calm his sister looked. With her hair tied up high and with flawless makeup, she smiled in his direction.

'Don't you cry, or I will,' she said, trying not to laugh.

'You look absolutely beautiful, sis. I mean it.'

'Thank you,' she said, looking at him up and down. 'You've scrubbed up well after the morning you've had.'

Not wanting to take the shine off his sister's day anymore, he decided to change the subject. 'You needed me?'

'Yes, I did,' she said. 'I'd like you to give me away.'

After the last few days he'd had, he hadn't even thought of the possibility of walking his sister down the aisle. He immediately replied, 'Of course I would love to.'

'Thank you.'

Looking at Samantha who was sitting on the edge of the bed with a stressed look on her face, Jess asked, 'Hey, Sam, I'm feeling a slight headache coming on. Do you have any Panadol?'

Sam closed her eyes and held her hands to her temple. With a notepad full of notes sitting on her lap, she replied, 'Uhh yes, probably in my mirrored cabinet in the ensuite Nick,' she said, pointing in the direction of the dressing room.

'On it,' he replied.

Walking through the dressing room, he was shocked at how large it was. He came into an expansive bathroom with sage green tiles on the floor and intricate black-and-white pattern tiles adorning the walls; the feature being a giant double shower with matching copper-plated waterfall shower heads.

He looked over towards the vanity and, seeing the makeup supplies on the left-hand side, decided to try the left-hand mirrored cabinet first. Pulling the door back and starting on the top shelf, he ran his eyes over the makeup supplies and toiletries, finally settling on the Panadol on the top shelf. Grabbing the small silver packet, he popped two small capsules out and dropped them on the counter. As he went to close the mirrored door, the sunlight coming through the large bay window shone on something in the cabinet causing it to sparkle directly into his eyes.

Adjusting his head slightly to get the reflection out of his eyes, he looked down at the loose jewellery sitting in a white dish on the bottom shelf of the white cabinet.

Sitting in the centre was his mother's wedding ring.

Chapter Thirty-Five

Nick's blood went cold and the world around him slowly melted away. He should've known it from the beginning. Russell Waterford had killed his mother. He had lied to him in the east sheds, and he lied to him in the interview room. He was so angry that he had begun to shake. He picked up the tiny unmistakable ring and slid it into his suit jacket pocket, feeling tears beginning to well in his eyes.

He realised that if he sent another email to the state DNA archives, he would once again be able to get an answer on the identity of his mother's killer.

Hearing movement in the dressing room, his sister called out, 'How did you go?'

Quickly wiping away his tears, he replied while smiling. 'Yup, got them here.'

He walked out of the ensuite and into the sitting room, passing his sister the two small capsules. As she swallowed them down, she noticed the change in body language in her brother.

'Are you ok?' she said, with a worried look on her face.

'I've never, ever been better,' he said with finality.

Standing outside the white picket fence with his sister with the crowd turned in their direction, he beamed as he walked Jess down the aisle.

Watching the nuptials from the front row, he sat hand in hand with Jemma, and was counting down the hours until the next day when he could get back to the station, and submit Russell Waterford's DNA in for his mother's cold case.

After the ceremony and during the reception, he began to wonder just how much Samantha Waterford knew about Russell's involvement in his mother's death.

With no alcohol or painkillers in his system for the first time in a while, he had never felt more clear headed. His mind was set on finally getting the answer. The only answer to the question he had ever truly wanted: who had killed his mother.

After the dancing had finally died down and guests began to leave, Nick and Jemma sat under the festoon lights in the warm night air, enjoying each other's company as the catering crew began to clean up around them.

Seeing Samantha Waterford for the first time since the ceremony, he watched the elderly matriarch with a wine glass in hand talk to the catering staff. One of the young men asked where best to put the rubbish. 'I'll take those bags over to the machinery shed over there,' she said, pointing at the small shed beside the house. 'Just put the rest where I start the pile.'

Sensing an opening where he could ask her some questions, Nick got up and joined the conversation. 'Here Samantha, I'll give you a hand.'

'Oh, Nick,' she replied, looking at him. 'Yes. That would be great, thanks.'

Walking over the gravel driveway and into the darkness, the unlikely couple headed towards the bright light shining from inside the shed. Making their way in next to the large tractor, Samantha dropped her bin bag against the back wall of the shed.

'Here will do, Nick,' she said, pointing at her bags.

He dropped his bags in the same spot and, then in a swift movement, pulled his mother's wedding ring out of his top pocket. 'What do you know about this ring?' he asked innocently, holding the ring up in front of her.

He had never seen a face change the way that Samantha did in that moment. Her smile subsided and her face went blank, with a blackness in her eyes. 'You know Nick, it's actually a relief,' she said, with a harshness in her tone he had never heard before.

'What is?' he replied, unsure where the conversation was going.

'I killed your mother,' Samantha said casually, finishing the remnants of her wine and placing it on the running board of the tractor.

He looked at the elderly woman and felt all the mis-aligned threads and connectors in his brain light up at once. Russell's love of Billie... and Samantha's jealousy... the missing ring... everything. It all made sense.

'Russell was obsessed with your mother,' she said. 'He never stopped talking about her, even after she had you and Jess; he would go on and on and on, "*Billie's great at tennis you should play. Billie's working at the service station, you should get a job.*" It was relentless, and I was sick of it.'

He stayed silent, feeling his skin beginning to crawl all over.

'Women were dying in towns all over the region,' she said, speaking of Jim Hooper's reign of terror. 'I knew what I was going to do, and I knew that with Hooper running around, if I did it like he did, I would get away with it,' she finished. 'God, It's such a relief to get it off my chest.'

Nick felt a burning rage simmering inside him. She had ruined his childhood and ruined so many lives by cutting his mother's short prematurely. He was so angry he couldn't find all the words he wanted to scream at the elderly woman. She had lived a long and full life, full of love and family. Something that she had cruelly taken away from him, his father, and his sister.

Unable to even form the words in his head, he grabbed her hard on her boney left wrist and spun her around, pushing her face much harder than he needed to, into the side of the giant tractor tyre beside them.

'Nick, you're hurting me!' she yelled, trying to squirm out of his grasp.

He felt the rage in his body slowly begin to lift, and it was replaced by a form of relief and satisfaction he had never felt in his whole life. He reached over onto the dusty workbench and grabbed a black cable tie, then wrapped it around her wrists nice and tight, and said words he had thought may never come out of his mouth.

'Samantha Waterford, you're under arrest for the murder of Billie Vada. You do not have to say or do anything, but if you do, it may be used in evidence against you.'

Chapter Thirty-Six

1992

Samantha sat in Russell's office, eating a chicken and salad roll for afternoon tea while her husband spoke to her. 'You know Sam,' he said, wiping mayonnaise from his mouth with the back of his shirt sleeve. 'I was speaking with Billie at the tennis club last night. She said if you wanted to join a team, you'd be more than welcome to.'

Of course, she did the smug bitch, Samantha thought to herself, blood boiling, picturing herself being beaten time and time again by her husband's true love.

'You know I don't play tennis Russ; I have young Pete to look after,' she said, nodding at her young son sitting in the corner of the office playing with a toy tractor. They were in the middle of a heatwave. A regional record, they had had five continual days over forty degrees, she was irritable and she thought she might just melt.

Russell sipped his can of diet Coke and kept going. 'I know Sam, but God, you should see her on the court!' he said fondly, as he looked down at his lunch. 'She's incredible,' he said finally.

Samantha felt something finally break inside her. After years of being told she was second best, she knew that something had to be done so she could be rid of Billie Vada once and for all, and she began to formulate a plan inside her head.

After reading the relentless news coverage of the 'Murray River Serial Killer' who was continuing to evade police, she made up her mind. Shipping Pete off with Russell for the weekend, she leant against her kitchen bench in quiet contemplation, and watched the blazing sun fall behind the gumtrees on her property.

The last sunset she will ever see, Samantha thought to herself. No longer will she constantly be made second best. While she may have won Russell's hand in marriage, Samantha knew that until she was rid of Billie, she would always be a consolation prize.

She had overheard a conversation during dinner at the pub the night before, about Tim Vada and Gary Jones going off on a shooting trip. As darkness fell, she knew that tonight would be the perfect opportunity. Grabbing the long hunting knife from

Russell's office in the east sheds, she made her way into town, making sure she didn't go over the speed limit or alert authorities in any way.

Dressed all in black, she parked at the far end of Evans Street and switched off her car. Looking at the illuminated clock on her dashboard, it read 11:13pm. Everyone should be asleep, she thought.

Reaching over into the passenger footwell, she grabbed Russell's oldest pair of boots and put them on her small feet, tying the laces as tight as she could.

Making her way silently along the footpath, she looked up into the night sky. Dark rolling clouds covered the moon, and aided her entry to the small weatherboard house at the end of the street. She held the knife tight in her small hand and looked down at the sharpened blade. After years, she knew it was time; time to finally stand up for herself, and never be second best again.

Walking up the driveway and over the lawn, she tiptoed silently up to the screen door, smiling to herself as she pulled it back and turned the handle of the front door. She knew it would be open.

Walking down the darkened hallway, she made her way towards the back of the house where she knew the master bedroom was, hoping to catch Billie in her sleep and end her own nightmare once and for all. Walking into the dimly lit dining room, she noticed light coming from the kitchen and made her way towards it.

At that moment, Billie Vada walked through the door with a glass of wine in her hand, and opened her mouth in shock.

'Jesus Christ, Samantha,' she whispered. 'What are you doing here? You scared the.'

Samantha didn't give her time to finish her sentence, lunging wildly with the knife in her direction with as much force as she could muster. Billie dodged the blade and threw her wine glass at Samantha. While trying to dodge the glass, Sam kicked a dining chair over and smashed the edge of her hip on the sharp corner of the dining table. She could feel warm blood trickle down her side.

The searing pain in her hip caused her anger to rise to a crescendo, and she lunged again at Billie, pushing her backwards through the door opening into the kitchen and the other woman's fingernails left deep scratch marks in the architrave as they went.

Billie fell backwards in, and Samantha watched as she smashed her head hard on the kitchen floor, causing her to lose consciousness. Samantha picked up the knife she had dropped and grabbed Billie by the feet, dragging her body the short distance into her master bedroom. With sheer adrenaline and surprising even herself, she managed to get the young woman up and onto the bed.

The motion of falling onto the bed woke Billie up and she looked up into Samantha's eyes with a deep sense of panic. The large hunting knife was hovering above her and she yelled. 'Samantha, what are you doing?! Please don't do this!'

Samantha pushed her hand hard down on Billie's neck and then stabbed down into her chest with as much force as she could muster. Feeling the blade penetrate deep in her chest, Samantha stabbed again and again as hard as she could, with tears streaming down her face.

'Stay away from my husband!' she yelled as she watched blood begin to pool out from underneath Billie's body and begin to cover her arms.

Lying on top of the body, she watched as the life left Billie Vada's eyes. Feeling her own body begin to quiver in shock, she realised what she had just done, and the adrenaline began to wear off. Moving off the bed, she made her way back through the kitchen and hallway, looking back at the bloodstained footprints she had created. Satisfied she had done her best to imitate the serial killer she had been reading so much about, she walked out of the front door and looked up at the now moonlit front yard. As her footsteps crunched across the gravel driveway, she felt like a weight had finally lifted off her shoulders.

Chapter Thirty-Seven

Nick sat on the front porch of his childhood home and read the small newspaper story in the bottom left-hand corner of page three of 'The Milford Times'.

Local Cold Case Finally Solved –

Thanks to the hard work of local police and with help from detectives from Sydney's homicide squad, the thirty year old murder of local woman, Billie Vada, has finally been solved.

A local woman has been arrested and is expected to be charged with the murder in the coming days.

More to come.

He smiled down at the tiny article and sipped his morning coffee, looking out at his old lawn, noticing small patches of green beginning to come through. He saw the white Milford police Landcruiser pull up to the kerb.

Watching the young senior constable hop out of the car, he laughed to himself. That car was really much too big for her, he thought. She could barely see over the steering wheel. It was ridiculous.

'Good morning,' Joanna said, standing on his nearly green lawn in her neat uniform.

'Good morning.'

'So, what now?' she asked.

'I'm going to enjoy my morning in Milford, for one of the first times since I got here.'

'And then?'

'I'm in no rush,' he said, sipping from his coffee.

'Well, if you are looking for some work to do on your leave, I've just had a report called in from the Sarge that some of the local ducks have been a bit too adventurous, and have made their way down the main street. I've been requested to muster them up and help them find their way back to the river,' she said with a laugh.

'Sounds like the exact type of police work you should be doing in Milford.'

'We'll talk soon,' she said, waving, as she made her way back out the front gate.

'I'm sure of it.'

As he watched the Landcruiser drive off into the distance, he heard his phone ring. Leaning over the old timber table, he grabbed it.

'Detective,' Chief Inspector Mark Johnson greeted him.

'Hi Chief.'

'Heard you've been busy. Great work down there son, I know how much this meant to you. I'm proud of you.'

He felt his heart beat in his chest. Too much emotion for this early in the day, he thought. The Chief was like a second father to him.

'Thanks Chief,' he said. It was all he could muster in reply.

'Right, then.' The Chief was never one to wax lyrical. 'You're needed back here. I'll see you Monday,' he said and hung up the phone before Nick had a chance to answer. Looks like it, Nick thought.

As the sun began to set, he sat in his father's old ute, hearing the V8 engine steadily idling. 'Thank you, Dad,' he said, as he slowly backed the pristine vehicle into his father's garage for the last time. Switching off the ignition, he could still smell the heat of the extractors, and he heard the hot pipes ticking as they cooled in the quiet tin shed. Closing the garage door behind him, he looked up to see Jemma standing on the back lawn, smiling at him.

'Hi.'

'Hey Jem.'

'You're leaving, aren't you?'

'I am.'

She walked up to him, held both of his hands, and looked into his eyes. 'Thank you for everything.'

'I'll be back.'

'I hope so,' she said with tears in her eyes.

He closed the old house for the last time, unsure of what he was going to do with it. When he asked his sister Jess, she told him he could have it. He could use it as a holiday house, she said, as she laughed at his foul expression.

Locking the front and screen doors and walking to the edge of the front deck, he turned left and turned off the sprinkler, which was cascading cool water over the front lawn. He'd done his best, he thought, looking at the patches of new green grass. But he knew it wouldn't last without proper care.

Walking out the front gate with his bag in hand, he turned back and looked at his childhood home, and thought of all the horrors that had happened inside the old building. There were new memories to be made in there too, he knew, and he hoped someone could do just that.

Cruising down the highway and back past the bullet-ridden 10 km sign, he looked over at the bright yellow canola crops for the last time, without a care in the world.

The End

Thank you so much for reading my novel

If you enjoyed *Warranilla*, make sure you check out the other titles in the Nick Vada series I have been writing – *Into The Flames, The Storm, The Kooleybuc Hotel, The Last Sunset and Murder In Secret*. They are all out now.

Also, if you enjoyed my novel, please consider leaving a rating/review on my Amazon book page or on Goodreads. It means a lot to hear what my readers think as reviews are hard to come by and I personally read every review.

Jason Summers

Printed in Great Britain
by Amazon

44996819R00199